P9-CEI-815

The Ayyar memory in Naill grew stronger; the change was almost complete. He could feel that behind him snuffed and ran—not the hounds—but things that were not yet men, that held only the rough, outward seeming of men. He knew, with a knowing from a consciousness he did not understand, that he had to reach Iftcan before the dreaded Larsh gathered for the final test of strength against strength—of life against life.

And he knew that as Ayyar or Naill, much more than his own survival depended on it....

JUDGMENT ON JANUS

Andre Norton

FAWCETT CREST • NEW YORK

JUDGMENT ON JANUS

THIS BOOK CONTAINS THE COMPLETE TEXT OF
THE ORIGINAL HARDCOVER EDITION.

Published by Fawcett Crest Books, a unit of CBS Publica-
tions, the Consumer Publishing Division of CBS Inc., by
arrangement with Harcourt Brace Jovanovich.

ISBN: 0-449-24214-5

Printed in the United States of America

First Fawcett Crest printing: December 1979

10 9 8 7 6 5 4 3 2 1

ONE · · THE STUFF OF DREAMS

Here even the sun was cold, just a glitter of light to hurt the eyes and reveal the square, sullen blocks of the Dipple. Naill Renfro leaned his forehead against the chill surface of the window, trying not to think—not to remember—to beat down those frightening waves of rage and frustration that brought a choking sensation into his throat these past few days, a stone heaviness to his chest.

This was the Dipple on the plant of Korwar—the last refuge, or rather prison, for the planetless flotsam of a space war. Forced from their home worlds by battle plans none of them had had a voice in framing, they had been herded here years ago. Then, when that war was over, they discovered there was no return. The homes they could remember were gone—either blasted into uninhabitable cinders through direct action, or signed away at conference tables so that other settlers now had "sole rights" there. The Dipple was a place to rot, another kind of death for those planted arbitrarily within its walls. A whole generation of spiritless children was growing up in it, to which this was the only known way of life.

But for those who could remember...

Naill closed his eyes. Limited space, curved walls, the endless throb of vibrating engines driving a Free Trader along uncharted "roads" of space, bright, exciting glimpses of strange worlds, weird creatures, new peoples—some alien of mind and body, some resembling the small boy who lurked unobtrusively in the background, drinking in avidly all the wonders of a trade meeting ...these he could remember. Then confusion—fear, which formed a cold lump in a small stomach, a sour taste in throat and mouth—lying in the cramped berth space of an escape boat with warm arms about him—the shock of the thrust-away from the ship that had always been his home—the period of drift while a mechanical signal broadcast their plight—the coming of the cruiser to pick them up as the only survivors. Afterwards—the Dipple—for years and years and years—always the Dipple!

But there had been hope that the war would end soon, that when he was big enough, old enough, strong enough, he could sign on a Free Trader, or that they would somehow find credit deposits owed to Duan Renfro and buy passage back to Mehetia. Wild dreams both those hopes had been. The dull, dusty years had wasted them, shown them to be flimsy shadows. There was only the Dipple, and that would go on forever—from it there was no escape. Or, if there was for him, not for her—now.

Naill wanted to cover his ears as well as close his eyes. He could shut out the grayness of the Dipple; he could not shut out now that weary little plaint, half croon, half moan, sounding monotonously from the bed against the far wall. He swung away from the window and came to stand at the side of the bed, forcing himself to look at the woman who lay there.

She—she was nothing but a frail wraith of skin and bones, not Malani.

Naill wanted to beat his fists against the gray wall, to cry out his hurt and rage—yes, and fear—as might a small child. It was choking him. If he could only gather her up, run away from this place of eternal harsh light, cold grayness. It had killed her, as much as Duan Renfro's death. She was withered by the ugliness and the hopelessness of the Dipple.

But instead of giving way to the storm within him, Naill knelt beside the bed, caught those restless, ever-weaving hands in his own, bringing their chill flesh up against his thin cheeks.

"Malani—" He called her name softly, hoping against all hope that this time she would respond, know him. Or was it far more kind not to draw her back? Draw her back—Naill sucked in his breath—there was a way for Malani to escape! If he were just sure, overwhelmingly sure that no other road existed....

Gently he put down her hands, pulled the covering up about her shoulders. Once sure... He nodded sharply, though Malani could not see that gesture of sudden decision. Then he went swiftly to the door. Three strides down the corridor and he was rapping on another door.

"Oh—it's you, boy!" The impatient frown on the woman's broad face smoothed. "She's worse?"

"I don't know. She won't eat, and the medico..."

The woman's lips shaped a word she did not say. "He's said she ain't got a chance?"

"Yes."

"For once he's right. She don't want any chance—you gotta face that, boy."

What else had he been doing for the past weeks! Naill's hands were fists against his sides as he fought down a hot response to that roughly kind truth.

"Yes," he returned flatly. "I want to know—how soon...?"

The woman swept back a loose lock of hair, her eyes suddenly bright and hard, locking fast to his in an unasked question. Her tongue showed between her lips, moistened them.

"All right." She closed the door of her own quarters firmly behind her. "All right," she repeated as if assuring herself in some way.

But when she stood beside Malani, she was concerned, her hands careful, even tender. Then she once more drew up the covers, looked to Naill.

"Two days—maybe a little more. If you do it—where's the credits coming from?"

"I'll get them!"

"She—she wouldn't want it that way, boy."

"She'll have it!" He caught up his over-tunic. "You'll stay until I come back?"

The woman nodded. "Stowar is the best. He deals fair—never cuts..."

"I know!" Naill's impatience made that answer almost explosive.

He hurried down the corridor, the four flights of stairs, out into the open. It was close to midday, there were few here. Those who had been lucky enough to find casual labor for the day were long since gone; the others were in the communal dining hall for the noon meal. But there were still those who had business in certain rooms, furtive business.

Korwar was, except for the Dipple, a pleasure planet. Its native population lived frankly to provide luxurious and entertaining living for the great and the wealthy of half a hundred solar systems. And in addition to those luxuries and pleasures, there were the fashionable vices, forbidden pleasures fed by smuggled and outlawed merchandise. A man could, if he were able to raise the necessary credits, buy into the Thieves' Guild and become a member of one of those supply lines. But there was also a fringe of small dealers who grabbed at the crumbs the Thieves' captains did not bother to touch.

They lived precariously, dangerously, and they

were recruited from the hopelessly reckless—from the Dipple dregs. Pleasures of a kind could be bought from such as Stowar. Pleasures—or a way of easy dying for a beaten and helpless woman.

Naill faced the pale boy lounging beside a certain doorway, met squarely the narrow eyes in that rat-mouthed countenance. He said only a name: "Stowar."

"Business, boot?"

"Business."

The boy jerked a thumb over his shoulder, rapped twice on the door.

"Take it, boot."

Naill pushed open the door. He felt like coughing; the smoke of a hebel stick was thick and cloying. There were four men sitting on cushions about a bros table playing star-and-comet, the click of their counters broken now and then by a grunt of dissatisfaction as some player failed to complete his star.

"What's the blast?" Stowar's head lifted perhaps two inches. He glanced at Naill, acknowledging his presence with that demand. "Go on—spout it—we're all mates here."

One of the players giggled; the other two made no sign they heard, their attention glued to the table.

"You have haluce—how much?" Naill came to the point at once.

"How much do you want?"

Naill had made his calculation on the way over. If Mara Disa could be relied upon, one pack ... no, better two, to be safe.

"Two packs."

"Two packs—two hundred credits," Stowar returned. "Stuff's uncut—I give full measure."

Naill nodded. Stowar was honest in his fashion, and you paid for that honesty. Two hundred credits. Well, he hardly expected to have it for less. The stuff was smuggled, of course, brought in from off-world by some crewman who wanted to pick up extra funds and was willing to run the risk of port inspection.

"I'll have it—in an hour."

Stowar nodded. "You do that, and the stuff's yours.... My deal, Gram."

Naill breathed deeply in the open, driving the fug from his lungs. There was no use going back to their own room, turning over their miserable collection of belongings to raise twenty credits— let alone two hundred. He had long ago sold everything worthwhile to bring in the specialist from the upper city. No, there was only one thing left worth two hundred credits—himself. He began to walk, his pace increasing as he went, as if he must do this swiftly, before his courage failed. He was trotting when he reached that other building set so conveniently and threateningly near the main gate of the Dipple—the Off-Planet Labor Recruiting Station.

There were still worlds, plenty of them, where cheap labor was human labor, not imported machines which required expert servicing and for which parts had to be planeted in at ruinous shipping rates. And such places as the Dipple were forcing beds for that labor. A man or woman could sign up, receive "settlement pay," be shipped out in frozen sleep, and then work for freedom—in five years, ten, twenty. On the surface that was a way of escape out of the rot of the Dipple. Only—frozen sleep was chancey: there were those who never awoke on those other worlds. And what awaited those who did was also chancey—arctic worlds, tropical worlds, worlds where men toiled under the lash of nature run wild. To sign was a gamble in which no one but the agency ever won.

Naill came to the selector, closed his eyes for a long moment, and then opened them. When he put his hand to that lever, pulled it down, he would take a step from which there would be no returning—ever.

An hour later he was once more at Stowar's. The star-and-comet game had broken up; he found the smuggler alone. And he was glad that was so as he put down the credit slip.

"Two fifty," Stowar read. From beneath the table he brought a small package. "Two here—and you get fifty credits back. Signed up for off-world?"

"Yes." Naill scooped up the packet, the other credit slip.

"You coulda done different," Stowar observed.

Naill shook his head.

"No? Maybe you're right at that. There're two kinds. All right, you got what you wanted—and it's all prime."

Naill's pace was almost a run as he came back to the home barracks. He hurried up the stairs, down the corridor. Mara Disa looked up as he breathlessly entered.

"The medico was here again—Director sent him."

"What did he say?"

"The same—two days—maybe three...."

Naill dropped down on the stool by the table. He had believed Mara earlier; this confirmation should not have made that much difference. Now he unrolled the package from Stowar—two small metal tubes. They were worth it—worth selling himself into slavery on an unknown world, worth everything that might come to him in the future... because of what they held for the dying woman who was his mother.

Haluce—the powder contained in one of those tubes—was given in a cup of hot water. Then Malani Renfro would not lie here in the Dipple; she would be reliving for a precious space of time the happiest day of her life. And if the thin thread that held her to this world had not broken by the time she roused from that sleep, there was the second draught to be sure. She had had to live in terror, defeat, and pain. She would die in happiness.

He looked up to meet Mara's gaze. "I'll give her this." He touched the nearer tube. "If—if there is need—you'll do the other?"

"You won't be here?"

That was the worst—to go and not to know, not to be sure. He tried to answer and it came out of him in a choked cry. Then he mastered himself to say slowly, "I—I ship out tonight.... They've given me two hours.... You—you'll swear to me that you'll be with her...? See"—he unrolled the slip for fifty credits—"this—take this and swear it!"

"Naill!" There was a spark of heat in her eyes. "All right, boy, I'll swear it. Though we don't have much to do with any of the old gods or spirits here, do we? I'll swear—though you need not ask that. And I'll take this, too—because of Wace. Wace, he's got to get out of here...not by your road, either!" Her hands tightened convulsively on the credit slip. Naill could almost feel the fierce determination radiating from her. Wace Disa would be free of the Dipple if his mother could fight for him.

"Where did you sign for?" she asked as she went to heat the water container.

"Some world called Janus," he answered. Not that it mattered—it would be a harsh frontier planet very far removed from the Dipple or Korwar, and he did not want to think of the future.

"Janus," Mara repeated. "Never heard of that one. Listen, boy, you ain't ate anything this morning. I got some pattercakes, made 'em for Wace. He musta got labor today, he ain't come back. Let me—"

"No—I'm shipping out, remember." Naill managed a shadow smile. "Listen, Mara, you see to things—afterwards—won't you?" He looked about the room. Nothing to be taken with him; you didn't carry baggage in a freeze cabin. Again he paused to master his voice. "Anything here you can use—it's yours. Not much left—except..." He went directly to the box where they had kept their papers, their few valuables.

His mother's name bracelets and the girdle Duan had traded for on Sargol were long since gone. Naill sorted through the papers quickly.

Those claim sheets they had never been able to use—might as well destroy them; their identity disks...

"These go to the Director—afterwards. But there's this." Naill balanced in his hand Duan Renfro's master's ring. "Sell it—and see... she has flowers... she loves flowers... trees... the growing things..."

"I'll do it, boy."

Somehow he was certain Mara would. The water was steaming now. Naill measured a portion into a cup, added the powder from the tube. Together they lifted Malani's head, coaxed her to swallow.

Naill again nestled one of the wasted hands against his cheek, but his eyes were for the faint curve of smile on those blue lips, the tinge of happiness which was a gossamer veil over the jutting of the cheekbones, the sharp angles of chin and jaw. No more moaning—just now and then a whisper of a word or a name. Some he knew, some were strange, out of a past he had not shared. Malani was a girl again, back on her home world of shallow seas beaded with rings and circles of islands, where tall trees rustled in the soft breeze that always came in late spring. Willingly she had traded that for life on a ship, following Duan Renfro out into the reaches of space, marrying a man who called no world, but a ship, home.

"Be happy." Naill put down her hand. He had given her all he had left to give, this last retracing—past care, sorrow, and the unforgivable present—into her treasured past.

"You there—you Naill Renfro?"

The man in the doorway wore the badged tunic of the Labor Agency, a stunner swung well to the fore at his belt. He was a typical hustler—one of the guards prepared to see the catch on board the waiting transport.

"I'm coming." Nail gently adjusted the blanket, got to his feet. He had to go fast, not looking back, never looking back now. But he halted to rap on Mara's door.

"I'm going," he told her. "You will watch?"

"I'll watch. And I'll do all the rest—just like you'd want it. Good luck, boy!" But it was plain that she thought that last a wasted wish.

Naill walked for the last time down the hall, trying to make his mind a blank, or at least hold to the thought that Malani was out of the Dipple in another way, a far better way. The guard gathered up two more charges and delivered them all at the processing section of the port. Naill submitted without question to the procedure that would turn him from a living, breathing man into a helpless piece of cargo, valuable enough once it was delivered intact and revived. But what he carried with him into the sleep of the frozen was the memory of that shadow smile he had seen on his mother's face.

How long was that voyage, in what direction among the stars, and for what reason, save cargo carrying, Naill was never to know, or really care. That Janus was a frontier world was a fact, or else human labor would not be necessary there. But that was the sum total of his knowledge concerning it. And he was not awake to see the huge dark green ball grow on the pilot's vision plate, develop wide continents and narrow seas—the land choked with the dense green of forests, such forests as more civilized planets had long since forgotten could draw nourishment from the soil and darken most of the countryside.

The spaceport on which the cargo tailed down was a stretch of bare rockland, scarred and darkened by the years of flame lashing from arriving and departing ships. And extending irregularly from that center were the clearings made by the settlers.

Garths had been hacked out of the forest, bare spots in the dark green, a green with a hint of gray, as if on some of the wide leaves of those giant trees, the avid saplings, and the brush about them a film of silver had powdered. Men cleared fields, setting disciplined rows of their own plants criss-crossing in those holdings, with the logs of the forest hollowed, split, and otherwise forced into serving as shelters for the men who had downed them.

This was a war between man and tree, with here a runner of vine, there a thrust of bush, a sprout of sapling tonguing out to threaten a painfully cleared space. Always the forest waited... and so did that which was within the forest....

The men who fought that battle were grim, silent, as iron-tough as the trees, as stubborn as space-scoured metal. A hundred years earlier that war had begun—when the first Survey Scout had marked Janus for human settlement. One attempt had been made to conquer the world for man and had failed. Then these last off-worlders had come and stayed. But still the forest had been cleared only a little—a very little.

Settlers were moving portward from the scattered garths, gathering at the town they hated but which they had to endure as their link off-world. These were hard men, bound together by a stern, joyless, religious belief, and a firm self-confidence and determination, men who labored steadily through the daylight hours, who mistrusted beauty and ease as part of deadly sin, who forced themselves and their children, their labor slaves, into a dull pattern of work and worship. Such came now to buy fresh labor in order to fight the forest and all it held.

"This is the lot, garthmaster. Why should I hold back my wares?" The cargomaster of the spacer balanced lightly, his fists resting on his hips, a contemptuous light in his eyes. Beside the would-be customer he was wire slim and boyish in appearance.

"For forest biting, for fieldwork, you bring such as these?" His contempt was as great, but divided between the spaceman and his wares.

"Men who still have something to bargain with do not sign on as labor, as you well know, garthmaster. That we bring here any at all is something to marvel at."

The settler himself was quite different from the miserable company he now fronted. In an age when most males of Terran descent, no matter how remote from the home planet that strain might be, eradicated facial and body hair at its first appearance, this hulking giant was a reversion to a primitive day. A fan of dense black beard sprayed across his barrel chest masking his face well up on the cheekbones. More hair matted the backs of his wide hands. As for the rest of him, he was gray—his coarse fabric clothing, his hide boots, the cap pulled down over more bushy hair.

His basic speech was gutteral, with new intonations, and he walked heavily, as if to crush down some invisible resistance. Tall, massive, he resembled one of the trees against which he and all his kind had turned their sullen hatred, while the men before him seemed pygmies of a weaker species.

There were ten of those, still shaken by the process of revival, and none of them had ever been the garthmaster's match physically. Men without hope, as the cargomaster had pointed out, were labor-signers. And by the time they had reached that bottom in any port, they were almost finished already, both physically and mentally.

The settler glowered at each, his eyes seeming to strip the unfortunate they rested upon in turn, measuring every defect of each underfed body.

"I am Callu Kosburg—from the Fringe. I have forty vistas to clear before the first snow. And these—these are what you offer me! To get an hour's full labor out of any would be a gift from the

Sky!" He made a sign in the air. "To ask a load of bark for such...it is a sin!"

The cargomaster's expression was serious. "A sin, garthmaster? Do you wish to accuse me of such before a Speaker? Here—now? If so, I shall bring forward my proof—so many credits paid for sign-on fees, cost of transportation, freeze fees. I think you will find the price well within allowed bounds. Do you still say 'sin,' Garthmaster Kosburg?"

Kosburg shrugged. "A manner of speaking only. No, I make no charge. I do not doubt that you could bring your proof if I did. But a man must have hands to help him clear—even if they are these puny crawlers. I will take this one—and this—and this." His finger indicated three in the labor line. "Also—you." For the first time he spoke directly to one of the laborers on view. "Yes, you—third man from the end. What age have you?"

Naill Renfro realized that demand was barked in his direction. His head still light, his stomach upset by the concoction they had poured into him, he struggled to make a sensible answer.

"I don't know—"

"You don't know?" Kosburg echoed. "What sort of an empty head is this one, that he does not even know how many years he has? I have heard much foolishness spoken here by off-worlders, but this is above all."

"He speaks the truth. According to the records, garthmaster, he was space-born—planet years do not govern such."

Kosburg's beard rippled as if he chewed his

words before spitting them out. "Space-born—
so.... Well, he looks young enough to learn how to
work with his hands. Him I will take, also. These
are all full-time men?"

The cargomaster grinned. "For such a run—to
Janus—would we waste space on less? You have
the bark ready for loading, garthmaster?"

"I have the bark. We shall put it in the loading
area. To be on the road quickly, that is necessary
when one travels to the Fringe. You—before me—
march! There is unloading to be done—though by
the looks of you, not much will pass by your
muscles this day."

The spaceport of Janus was a cluster of prefabs
about the scorched apron of the landing field,
having the strangely temporary look of a rootless
place, ugly with the sterile starkness of the Dipple.
Urged by a continuous rumble of orders, the
laborers hurried to a line of carts. Their cargoes,
unwieldly bundles of silvery bark, were being
transferred by hand to growing stacks carefully
inspected by a ship's tallyman.

"This—goes there." Kosburg's simple instruc-
tions were made with waves of his hand indicating
certain carts and the bark piles. Naill looked up at
the man standing in the nearest wagon, balancing
a roll of bark to hand down.

He was a younger edition of Kosburg. There was
no mistaking they were father and son. The beard
sprouting on his square thrust of chin was still
silky, and the lips visible above it pouted. Like his
father, he was dressed in heavy, ill-fitting gray
clothing. In fact all the men working along that

line of rapidly emptying wagons presented a uniformity of drabness that was like some army or service garb.

But Naill had little chance to note that, for the bundle of bark slid toward him and he had just time to catch it. The stuff was lighter than it looked, though the size of the roll made it awkward to manage. He got it to the stack safely in spite of the unsteadiness of his feet.

Three such journeys brought him back to an empty cart. And he stood still, with a chance to look about him.

Two heavy-shouldered, snorting beasts were harnessed to each of the wagons. Broad flat hind feet and haunches were out of proportion to their slim front legs, which ended in paws not unlike his own hands. They sat back on those haunches while, with the hand paws, they industriously scratched in the hairy fur on their bellies. In color they were a slaty blue with manes of black—a dusty black—beginning on their rounded, rodent-like skulls, and running down to the point end of their spines. They had no vestige of tail. Wide collars about their shoulders were fastened in turn to the tongue of the cart by a web of harness, but Naill could see no control reins.

"In!" Kosburg's hairy hand swept past his nose. And Naill climbed into the now empty wagon.

He settled down on a pile of rough sacking, which still gave forth the not unpleasant odor of the bark. Two of his fellow immigrants followed him, and the back of the cart was locked into place by the garthmaster.

The son, who had not uttered a word during the unloading, occupied the single raised seat at the front of the wagon. Now he raised a pole to rap smartly in turn the two harnessed scratchers. They complained in loud snorts, but moved away from the port strip, their pace between a hop and a walk, which made the cart progress unevenly in a fashion not comfortable for passengers. One of the men was promptly and thoroughly sick, only managing to hang over the tailboard in time.

Naill studied his companions dispassionately. One was big, even if he was only a bony skeleton of the man he must once have been. He had the greenish-brown skin of a former space crewman and the flat, empty eyes of one who had been on more than one happy-dust spree. Now he simply sat with his shoulders planted against the side of the cart, his twitching hands hanging between his knees, a burned-out hulk.

The one who had been sick still leaned against the tailboard, clawed fingers anchoring him to that prudent position. Fair hair grew sparsely on a round skull; his skin was dough-white. Naill had seen his like before, too. Some skulker from the port who had signed on for fear of the law—or because he had chanced to cross seriously a VIP of the underworld.

"You—kid—" The man Naill watched turned his head. "Know anything about this place?"

Naill shook his head. "Labor recruiter said Janus—agriculture." In spite of the jiggling process of the cart, he ventured to pull himself up, wanting a chance to see the countryside.

They were following a road of beaten bare earth, running between fenced fields. Naill's first impression was of somberness. In its way this landscape was as devoid of color and life as the blocks of the Dipple.

The plants in the fields were low bushes set in crisscross lines, while the fences which protected them were stakes of peeled wood set upright, a weaving of vines between them. Mile after planet mile of such fields—but, in the far distance, a dark smudge that might mark either hills or woodland.

"What's all that?" The man had moved away from the tailboard, edging around to join Naill.

Naill shrugged. "I don't know." They might be companions in exile here, but he had no liking for the other.

Small but very bright and knowing eyes surveyed him. "From the Dipple, ain't you, mate? Me—I'm Sim Tylos."

"Naill Renfro. Yes, I'm from the Dipple."

Tylos snickered. "Thought you was gonna get yourself a new start off-world, boot? The counters don't never run that way 'cross the table. You just picked yourself another hole to drop into."

"Maybe," Naill replied. He watched that smudge at the meeting of the drab, unhappy land with a sky that carried a faint tinge of green. Suddenly he wanted to know more about that dark line, approach it closer.

The hop-shuffle of the animals drawing the wagon was swift. And the group of five wagons, their own the leading one, was covering ground at a steady and distance-eating pace. Sim Tylos with

a lifted finger indicated the driver of their own
cart. "Suppose he'll talk a bit?"

"Ask him."

Naill let Tylos pass him but did not follow when
the other took his stand behind the driver's seat.

"Gentlehomo—" Tylos's voice was now a
placating whine. "Gentlehomo, will you—"

"Whatcha want, fieldman?" The younger Kosburg's basic was even more gutturally accented
than his father's.

"Just some information, gentlehomo—" Tylos
began. The other cut in: "Like where you're goin'
and what you'll be doin' there, fieldman? You're
going right on to the end of the fields—to the
Fringe, where like as not the monsters'll get you.
And what you'll be doin' there is good hard work—
'less you want the Speaker to set your sins hard on
you! See them there?" He flicked the end of his
encouragement pole at the bushes in the fields.
"Them's our cash crop—lattamus. You can't set
out lattamus till you have a bare field—no shoots,
no runners, nothin' but bare field. And on the
Fringe gettin' a bare field takes some doin'—a
mighty lot of axin', and grubbin', and cuttin'. We
aim to get us some good lattamus fields 'fore you
all go to account for your sinnin'.

" 'Course"—young Kosburg leaned over to stare
straight into Tylos's eyes—"there're some sinners
as don't want to aid the Clear Sky work—no, they
don't. And them has to be lessoned—lessoned
good. My sire back there—he's a good lessoner.
Speaker puts the Word on him to reckon with real
sinners. We're Sky People—don't hold with killin'

or such-like off-world sinnin'. But sometimes lessonin' sits heavy on hard-hearted sinner!"

Though his words might be obscure, his meaning was not. There was a threat there, one that young Kosburg took pleasure in delivering. Tylos shrank back, sidled away from the driver's seat. Kosburg laughed again and turned his back on the laborer. But Tylos now stood as still as the jolting of the wagon would let him, staring out over the countryside. When he spoke again, it was in a half whisper to Naill.

"Nasty lot—not by half, they ain't. Work a man—work him to death, more'n likely. This here's a frontier planet—probably only got one spaceport."

Naill decided the little man was thinking aloud rather than taking him into his confidence.

"Got to play this nice and easy—no pushing a star till you're sure you got a line on the comet's trail—no fast movin'. This lessonin' talk—that ain't good hearin'. Think they has us all right and tight, does they? Let 'em think it—just let 'em!"

Naill's head was aching, and the lurching of the cart was beginning to make him queasy. He sat down, across from the still-staring ex-spaceman, and tried to think. The agreement he had signed in the labor office—it had been quite detailed. So much advance—Naill's memory shied away violently from the thought of how that advance had been spent—so much for expenses, for shipment to this world. He had no idea of the value of the bark that Kosburg had paid for him, but that could be learned. By the agreement he should be able to repay that—be a free man. But how soon? Best settle down and learn what he could, keep eyes and ears open. The Dipple had been a static kind of death; this was a chance at something...what he had no idea, but he was hoping again.

Duan Renfro had been a Free Trader, born of a line of such explorers and reckless space rovers. Though Naill could hardly remember his father, some of the intuition and abilities of that unsettled and restless type were inherited qualities of mind and body. Malani Renfro was of a frontier world, though one as far different from Janus as sere autumn was from spring. She had been third generation from First Ship there, and her people had still been exploring rather than settling. To observe, to learn, to experiment with the new, were desires, needs, which had lain dormant in Naill growing up in the vise of the Dipple. Now that need awoke and stirred.

When they stopped for a meal of gritty bread and dried berries, Naill watched the beasts munching their fodder. The driver of the second cart was small and thin, a seamed scar of an old blaster burn puckering the side of his head, plainly another off-world laborer.

"What do you call them?" Naill asked him.

"Phas." His answer came in one word.

"Native here?" Naill persisted.

"No. They brought 'em—First Ship." He pointed with chin rather than hand to the Kosburgs.

"First Ship!" Naill was startled. He tried to remember the scant information on Janus. Surely the settlers had been established here longer than one generation.

"Came in twenty years ago. These Sky Lovers bought settlement rights from the Karbon Combine and moved in. Only the port's free land now."

"Free land...?"

"Free for off-worlders. Rest's all Sky Lovers' holdings—family garths—pushing out a little more each year." Again his chin pointed, this time to that dusky line on the horizon. "Gotta watch yourself 'round these phas. Look peaceful but they ain't always—not with strangers. They can use them teeth to crack up more'n a borlag nut, do they want to."

The teeth were long and white, startlingly so against the dark body fur of the animals, and very much on display. But the phas themselves appeared to be completely absorbed in eating and paid no attention to the men.

"Holla!" Kosburg, the elder, bellowed enough to excite even the phas. "Get them animals ready to move out. You"—his wave put Naill in motion back to his own wagon—"climb up."

As the afternoon wore on, the supply of lattamus bushes dwindled in the roadside fields. Here and there were patches of grain or vegetables, the fences about them of a lighter shade, as if they had weathered for only a short space of time.

And always that dusky shadow crept toward them... or that was the way Naill felt it moved—a shadow advancing toward the men and carts, not men and carts creeping up to it. Now it was clearly a dark forest wall of trees, and here were evidences that it had not been dispossessed easily. Vast stumps were in the fields, some of them smoking as if eaten by fires kept burning to utterly destroy them. Naill had a vision of the labor needed to win such a field from virgin forest, and he drew a deep breath of wonder.

He tried to put together what he guessed, and knew, about the garths, the men who worked them. Clothing, carts, the allusions in the speech of both Kosburgs and that of the laborer-driver led Naill to believe that this was a sect settlement. There had been many of those through the centuries after the first Terrans ventured into deep space and began their colonization of other worlds. Groups knit together by some strong belief sought out empty worlds on which to plant their private utopias undisturbed by "worldly" invaders. Some had become so eccentric as to warp life on them into a civilization totally alien to the past of the first settlers. Others liberalized, or dwindled forgotten, leaving only ruins and graves to mark vanished dreams.

Naill was uneasy. Farm labor would be back-breakingly hard. He had expected that. A fanatical belief was something else, a menace to such as he, which was, to his mind, worse than any natural danger on a strange planet. The Free Traders were also free believers, their cosmopolitan descents and occupations making for wide tolerance of men and ideas. The guiding spirit of Malani's home world, a kindly world, had been recognized by the worshipers there as a gentle and tolerant Power. The narrow and rigid molds some men set, to imprison their belief in a Force above and beyond their greatest human striving, were as much a danger to a stranger in their midst as a blaster in the hands of an open and avowed enemy. And now that sinister talk of "lessoning," which young Kosburg had used earlier, struck home to Naill.

He longed passionately for a chance to ask questions. But again such inquiries as he wanted to make might well bring down upon him the very attention he wished least to attract. Those questions—concerning religion and purpose—were oftentimes forbidden, even to the followers within the mold of a fanatical community. No—better to watch, listen, try to put the pieces together for himself now.

The wagon turned from the road into a narrower land and then passed the gate in a stake wall higher than any field partition, one that might have been erected as a defense rather than to mark a division between one section of land and the next. And their coming was greeted by a baying.

· Hounds—enough like the Terran animals that had borne that designation to be named so—a half dozen of them, running and leaping behind another and lower fence, were slavering out their challenge to the newcomers. Naill watched that display. What menace, living in the shadow of the now plainly visible forest, moved the garth dwellers to keep such a pack? Or—there was a chill between his shoulder blades, creeping down his spine—were those guards to keep workers like himself in line?

The carts pulled on into a hollow square, surrounded by buildings, and Naill forgot the hounds momentarily to gape at the main house of the garth. That—that—thing—was fully as tall as two stories of the Korwar Dipple, but it was a single tree trunk laid on its side, with windows cut in two rows, and a wide door of still-scaled bark. Why—the stumps he marveled at in the field were but the remains of saplings compared to this monstrosity! What kind of trees *did* make up the forests of Janus?

THREE   TREASURE TROVE

Naill leaned against the supporting haft of the big stripping ax. On his body, bare to the waist, silver dust was puddled into patches by sweat. Overhead the sun, which had seemed so pale on that first day of his arrival, proved its force with waves of heat. His head turned, as it so often had these past weeks, toward the cool green of the woods they were attacking. The dim reaches of dark green were as promising as a pool into which a man could plunge his sweating, heat-seared body—to relax, to dream.

Kosburg had lost no time, after their arrival at

this Fringe garth, in outlining to his new hands all
the dire dangers of that woodland which beckoned
so enticingly. And not the least of those perils was
marked by the solitary, ruined hut he had shown
them, well within one strip of forest that licked out
into his painfully freed acres—now cursed land,
which no man would dare to trouble. That hut—
they viewed it from a safe distance—had been, and
still was, the tomb of a sinner, one who had
offended so greatly against the Sky as to be struck
down by the Green Sick.

The Believers did not kill—no, they simply
abandoned to the chill loneliness of the forest
those who contracted that incurable disease,
which was sent to them as a punishment. And
what sufferer raving in the high fever of the first
stages could survive alone and untended in the
wild? Also—who knew what other dangers lurked
under the shadow of the great trees? There were
the monsters, seen from time to time, always
viewed in the early morning before the sun's
rising, or in the twilight.

Naill wondered about those "monsters." The
stories Kosburg's household related with a relish
were wild enough, but the creature or creatures
described were surely born from over-vivid imagi-
nations. The tales agreed only upon the fact that
the unknown was nearly the same color as the
vegetation wherein it sheltered and that it had four
limbs. As to whether it walked erect on two, or ran
on four, the information appeared to be divided.
And against it the hounds of the garths had an
abiding hate.

Curiosity was not one of the character traits the settlers either possessed in good supply or encouraged. Naill's first fears concerning the inbound quality of the society on Janus had been fully substantiated. The belief of the Sky Lovers was a narrow, fiercely reactionary one. Those living on the garths might well have stepped back a thousand years or more into the past history of their kind.

There was no desire to learn anything of the native Janus, only dogged, day-in, day-out efforts to tame the land, make it conform to their own off-world pattern of life. Where another type of settler would have gone exploring into the vastness of the forest lands, the Sky Lovers shunned the woods, except when armed with ax, lopping knife, shovel, and the thirst for breaking, chopping, digging.

"You—Renfro—bend to it!"

That was Lasja tramping into the half-hacked clearing, his own ax across his shoulder. He had been the longest in Kosburg's labor service and so took upon himself the hustling of the latest comers. Behind him came Tylos carrying a slopping water bucket, his face puckered in an attempt to act out the pain such a vast effort cost him.

The ex-crook from Korwar was striving to use every wile and trick he had learned in his spotted past to make life for himself as easy as he could. His first day at clearing had brought him back early to the garthstead with a swollen ankle from what Naill thought was a carefully calculated misstroke of a grubbing hook. Hobbling about the buildings, he then strove to ingratiate himself in

the kitchen and weaving house, his quick, sly
tongue as busy as his hands were slow, until the
womenfolk of Kosburg's establishment accepted
him as part of their aids to labor. So he escaped
the fields, though Naill, having heard the flay-
ing tongue of the mistress of the household in full
flap, doubted whether Tylos had won the better
part.

Now he leaned against the bole of a fallen tree
and smirked behind Lasja's broad back, winking
at Naill as the latter began to shape up one of the
waiting logs.

"Seen any of them monsters?" he asked as Naill
paused and came over for a drink. "Reckon their
hides might bring a good price down to the port,
was anyone smart enough to take him out a pair of
hounds and do a little huntin'."

His half suggestion only pointed up the thought
that was at the back of all newcomers' minds—the
driving hope of somehow managing to get some
trade goods independently, to build up credits at
the port and some day—no matter how far away—
to earn one's freedom.

Lasja scowled. "You stow that! Ain't never goin'
to get any trade goods—you know that, scuttle-
bug. Anything you get—or find—belongs to the
garthmaster—and don't you go to forget that!
Want to be judged a first-degree sinner and have
the Speaker reckon with you?"

Naill glanced over the rim of the wooden dipper.
"What could a man get—or find—around here,
Lasja, that's worth bringing in a Speaker?"

Lasja's scowl blackened. "Sinful things," he
muttered.

Naill allowed the dipper to splash back into the bucket. He was aware of Sim Tylos's sudden start, stilling instantly into watchful waiting. When the big man did not continue, it was Tylos who asked the question in both their minds.

"Sinful things, eh? And what're them, Lasja? We don't want to get no Speaker on our backs—better tell us what we ain't to pick up, if we are findin' of 'em. Or else, do we get into trouble, we can say as how we was never told no different. This Kosburg, he's a terror on two legs, all right, only he might listen to us sayin' somethin' like that."

Tylos was right. Stern and narrow as was the garthdwellers' creed, their sense of justice still worked—justice, not mercy, of course. Lasja paused, his ax still upraised. His lower lip pushed out so that he had the side profile of some awkward, off-world bird thing—round head, outthrust bill.

"All right—all right!" He brought down the ax mightily and then let the haft slip through his hand until the head rested on the chip-littered ground. "Sometimes, men workin' out to clear the forest—they find things...."

"What kind of things?" Naill took up the questioning.

But Lasja's discomfort was growing. "Things—well, you might say as how they was like treasures."

"Treasures!" Tylos broke out and then clamped his pale lips tightly together, though his avid interest blazed in his narrowed eyes.

"What kind of treasures?" Naill asked.

"I don't know—just things—rich-lookin'."

"What happens to 'em?" Tylos's tongue stopped its passage across his lips long enough for him to ask.

"The Speaker comes and they break 'em all to bits—burn 'em."

"Why?" Naill demanded.

"'Cause they're cursed, that's why! Anybody as touches 'em is cursed too."

Tylos laughed. "That's rich, that is. 'Course they're cursed, do we find 'em. We might just take 'em down to the port and buy ourselves free. But why smash 'em up? They could use some treasure here—import some machines so we don't have to go on breakin' our backs cuttin' down trees and grubbin' out stuff."

Lasja shot him a hard glance. "You ain't breakin' your back none, Tylos. And the Sky Lovers don't use no machines. Anyway—does a man try to hold out on treasure and they learn it, he gets put out there"—he jerked a thumb at the forest—"alone—no grub, no tools, nothin' but his bare hands. And you ain't sellin' nothin' at the port. You don't get to the port less'n they make sure they's nothin' a man's got on him but his clothes over his bare skin. No—they's right—that treasure's not for the takin'. When it's found, the finder sings out, and loud, too."

"Where does it come from? I thought this was an empty world, no native race," Naill said.

"Sure—never found no people here. Funny thing—I've heard a lotta talk. This here planet's been known for about a hundred years, planet time. The Karbon Combine bid it in at the first

Survey auction—just on spec. That was before the war—long before. But they didn't do much more than just hold it on their books—sent in a couple of explorin' parties who didn't see more'n trees, messes of trees all over the place. There's a couple of narrow little seas—all the rest forest. No minerals has registered high enough to pay for exportin'—nothin' but a lotta wood.

"Then, when it looked like the Combines were stretchin' too far, mosta them started unloadin' worlds what didn't pay—gettin' rid of 'em to settlers. These Sky Lovers—they were over on some hard-soiled scrap of an overbaked world which gave 'em a hardscrabble livin'. Somehow they got the down payment for Karbon and jumped the gulf to here. Then—when the war broke—well, then they had it made. Karbon holdin's were all enemy then—they cracked wide open and nobody came around here askin' for what was still owin'. Far's I know, the Sky Lovers have Janus free and clear all to their selves. They get out lattamus and bark enough to keep the port open and themselves on the trade map.

"That's all the history we know. And there's never been no sign of natives, just these treasures turnin' up every once in a while. No pattern to that neither, no ruins—nothin' to say as how there was ever anythin' here but trees. And those've been growin'—some of 'em—nigh onto two thousand planet years! Might just be that this was some sort of a hideout for raiders or such once. But they ain't never found no marks of a ship landin' neither. The Sky Lovers, they have it that the treasures are planted by the Dark One just to make a man sin, and so far they ain't found nothin' to prove that wrong."

Tylos laughed scornfully. "Silly way of thinkin'!"

"Maybe—but it's theirs and they've got the say here," Lasja warned.

"Did you ever really see any such treasure?" Naill went back to his stripping job.

"Once—over on Morheim's Garth. He's to the south, next holding. That was last fall, just when we was doin' the season burnin'. Was his son as found it. They had the Speaker in right away— rounded us all up for the prayin' and the breakin'. Didn't do 'em much good, though—only kinda proved their point about it bein' sinful."

"How?"

"'Cause just about a week of days later, that same son as found it—he came down with the Green Sick. They carted him off to the forest then. I was one of the guards they set for the watchin'."

"The watching?"

"Yeah. With the Green Sick they go plumb outta their heads—sometimes they run wild. Can't let 'em back where there's people. They touch you and you get it too. So if they try to break back, you rope 'em—pull 'em in and tie 'em to some tree."

"Leave sick people that way to die!" Naill stared at Lasja.

"There ain't nothin' as can be done for 'em—no cure at all. And the port medico says as how they could infect the whole lot of us. Sometimes their folks give 'em a sleep drink so they just die that way. But that ain't right, accordin' to the Speakers. They ought to be made known as how they's sinned. And, lissen here, boy, the Green Sick ain't nothin' to want—nor to look at neither. You ain't human no more, once it begins on you." Lasja chopped at the tree. "They say as how it never touches no one 'less he's broken some sorta rule of theirs—been different somehow. That Morheim boy—he was lessoned once or twice by his father, right out before the whole garth—for doin' wrong. So when he took sick, it was a judgment, like."

"You believe that?" Naill asked.

Lasja shrugged. "Seen it work that way—or heard as how it does. Them what takes the Green Sick, they's all had some trouble with the Rule. Once it was a girl as was kinda queer in the head— used to want to go into the forest, said as how she liked the trees. She got lessoned good for wanderin' off. Just a little thing she was, not full growed yet. They found her burnin' up in her bed place one night—took her right off to the woods. It weren't pretty—she cried a lot. And her mother—she was Kosburg's second woman—she took on somethin' awful. Old man had her locked up for a couple weeks—till he was sure it was all over."

Naill chopped savagely. "Why didn't they just kill her? Would have been kinder!"

Lasja grunted. "They don't figure so. Bein' kind to her body wouldn't save her spirit. She had to die hard in order to get rid of her sin. They think as if a man don't die in the Clear—as they calls it—he'll be in the Shadow always. If you sin big, you have to pay for it. Makes for a lot of hard dealin' one way

or another sometimes. You can't change their way
of thinkin' and it's best not to meddle. They hold
that lessonin's good for everyone, not just those
that believe. Now—we've had enough jawin'! You,
Tylos, make tracks with that bucket to the splittin'
ground. Tell the garthmaster as how we have a
load 'bout ready. And don't you linger none on the
way, neither."

Tylos, his bucket slopping, hurried as long as he
was in Lasja's sight. Probably that scuttle would
drop to a crawl as soon as he put a screen of brush
between them. Since the usually taciturn Lasja
seemed in an open-jawed mood, Naill determined
to make the most of the opportunity to learn what
he could.

"Lasja, has anyone ever bought free here?"

"Bought free?" The axman appeared to jerk out
of some private path of thought. He grinned. "You
needn't wear yourself out, boy, thinkin' 'bout that.
Iffen you can shoulder a phas and trot him twice
'round the garth—then you can think of buyin'
free. This is a dirt-poor world—and Kosburg's is an
outer-Fringe holdin'. He ain't goin' to let loose of
any pair of hands he gets. Not while they can still
work, that is. You're right puny, but you ain't no
shirk like Tylos. You do a day's work right enough.
Me—I was prisoner of war on Avalon. They came
'round to the camp and made labor offers. I took
that—better than stayin' in and goin' mad with
bein' cooped up. When I came here—sure, I had big
ideas about doin' my time and buyin' free. Only—
this is the way of it—all the land, every stinkin'

wood-rotten bit of it, belongs to the Sky, accordin'
to their reckonin'. And only a true Believer can get
rights to take up a garth. And—this is the trick star
in their game—you can't be no true Believer 'less
you was born so. They made them a pact, when
they took off from that mistake of a world where
they was roostin' before, that they wouldn't let in
no disturbin' outsiders with different ideas. So you
gotta be born a Believer, you can't up and say as
how you'd like to join 'em now.

"Once here, they've got you tighter'n an air-lock
door. You can go up against 'em and get yourself
lessoned—or maybe thrown out in the woods—but
they've got you just where it suits 'em! Now, you do
that there smoothin' down. We'd better have a fair
load for the old man when he comes sniffin'
'round."

How far were they from the port? A good day's
travel in one of the phas-drawn carts—maybe
longer on foot. And how could anyone work out an
escape even if he were able to reach that single tie
with space? To hire passage on a spacer would cost
indeed a "treasure"; to try to work some deal with
any ship's commander to be taken on as crew
would be useless. The sympathies of the officers
would all be with the master one was trying to
escape. And if there was no system of legal
buyfree ... Naill dug savagely with the point of his
ax against the hard wood. He hated to believe that
Lasja's gloomy report was the truth, but it sounded
likely.

"You take that rope." Lasja broke into his

assistant's train of discouraging thought. "And drag out another of them logs. You can plunk it 'bout here."

Naill put down the ax and went back into where the trees had been felled during the past two days. He was still out of the coverage of the full forest, but the mass of greenery, just beginning to wilt, was somehow refreshing. There was a different feel here to the land, smells that were aromatic, free from the taint of human living. On impulse he stripped off handfuls of silver-green leaves, their touch fur-soft against his damp skin as he held them close to his nose and drank in a spicy fragrance.

He was filled with a sudden desire to keep on going into the domain of the trees. What if a man did take to the woods? That would mean becoming an outlaw in unknown country. But was that state so much worse than garth life? His mind nibbled at that as he hunched down to knot the rope about a tree trunk. The twist of cordage cut cruelly into his shoulder on the first pull. There was resistance, too much. Naill knelt again, saw a branch had cut into a soft place in the ground and pinned the tree fast there.

With his lopping knife he set to work digging that free. Sunlight lay in ragged patches. And something blazed with leaping light where he dug. Naill clawed out loose handfuls of moist loam and uncovered what lay beneath.

He blinked. Lasja's stories had not prepared him for this. And truly—what was it? A figure of— was it a tree?—a ball, a box, a rod the length of his palm and perhaps two inches thick, a necklace spilling a circlet of green-fire droplets on the gray soil.

Naill's hand closed upon the rod, brought it into full sight.

He drew a deep breath of pure wonder. There had been so many years of drabness, of ugliness. And now he could not give name to what he held in his hand. The substance was cold, with the pleasant coolness of springwater cupped in a sweaty hand to be brought to a thirsty mouth. It was all light—green, gold, opaline—jeweled light. It was a form—in traceries of patterns—to entrance, to enchant the eyes. It was a fabulous wonder that was his! His!

Moved by some instinctive fear, Naill sat half crouched, looking about him. Smashed, burned— that was what Lasja said was done to such things! Sure—that was part of their narrow world. Break beauty, destroy it, as they broke and destroyed the beauty of the Forest. He had not the slightest hope of keeping the entire treasure: he had no desire to. But this rod—this tube with all its imprisoned, magic splendor—that was not going to be broken!

Lasja would be along any moment, and Naill had no doubt about the other's reaction. He'd call Kosburg at once. Where—where was a hiding place?

He balled his fist tightly about his treasure. The woods—perhaps he could find a place of concealment there. Naill got to his feet, stole into the shadow of the trees, and saw there on the bole of one a dark hole. He thrust the tube into that hollow just as Lasja called from close at hand.

Naill leaped, kicked soil back, took up the rope
to pull as the other came into view. He dared not
turn his head to see how much dirt his kicks had
replaced, whether he had again concealed the rest
of the treasure.

"You empty-skulled lackwit!" Lasja bore down
upon him. "Whatta you doin', pullin' out your guts
that way? You got a limb caught under that
thing!"

The older man went down on one knee to dig
with his lopping knife, just as Naill had done
before him. Then that busy arm paused. Lasja
tumbled away as if he had just laid hand on a
lurking jacata worm. He scrambled to his feet and
grabbed Naill, propelling him away from the tree.
And at the same time he gave a carrying call that
would summon Kosburg. It was plain Lasja was
obeying the Rule.

FOUR   SINNER

Tylos stood against the wall bunk, his hands
opening and closing as if he wanted to grab and
hold what was not there. He leaned toward Naill,
his pale tongue sliding back and forth across his
lips.

"You musta seen somethin'—you musta!
Treasure—what kinda treasure, man?"

They were all herded in the bunkhouse, the
dozen off-world laborers Kosburg had. And all
eleven pairs of eyes were on Naill. Only Lasja was
missing, kept behind as a guide. Naill hedged.

"Lasja dug it out—the tree branch was caught. I

was on the rope drag and he dug. Then he pushed me out of there and called Kosburg. I saw something shinning in the dirt—that's all."

"Why—why call Kosburg?" Tylos demanded of the company at large. "Treasure—get that down to the port, and any trader'd take if off your hands for enough to buy your passage out."

"No." Hannosa, never a talkative man and one of the older laborers, shook his head. "That's where you're off course, Tylos. No trader finning in on Janus would deal with one of us—he'd lose port license if he tried."

"Not the master, maybe," Tylos conceded. "But don't tell me the whole crew of every ship is gonna turn blind eye to a profitable little deal on the side. Lissen, dirt grubber, I come from Korwar—I know how much can be made outta treasure. Alien things—they bring big prices—big enough to make the cut worthwhile all along the line from a crewman up to the final seller in some fancy VIP place."

Hannosa continued to shake his head. "This is a matter of belief. And you know—or ought to know—that means a complete clampdown at any port. There've been five treasures found in the past three years—that we've heard about—in this district alone. Every one of them finished the same way—destroyed under careful supervision."

"Why?" Naill was the one to ask now. "Don't they realize that these finds are important?"

"To whom?" Hannosa retorted. "To the Sky Lovers their own creed and way of life is all-important. If news of such finds brings in strangers, archeologists, treasure seekers, then they would open the door to what these people came to Janus to escape: contact with other beliefs and customs. That mustn't happen, they think. As they see it, there is evil inherent in these objects—so they are destroyed."

"It ain't right!" Tylos pounded a small fist against the side of the bunk. "It purely ain't right to smash up stuff like that!"

"Go tell Kosburg that," one of the other men suggested. "Me—as long as we have to stay outta the fields till the Ceremony, I'm gonna get some rest." He stretched out on his bunk, setting an example most of the rest were quick to follow.

Tylos went to the window, though what he might be able to see from there Naill did not know. He himself lay flat and closed his eyes. But through his whole body there was a quiver of excitement so intense that he feared everyone in the room could sense it. Had he really done the impossible, kept for himself a fraction of that find? Had luck favored him that far?

When he closed his eyes, he could see vividly again that tube with its patterns, its color. And in his palm he could feel the sleekness of its substance. What was it? For what purpose had it been fashioned? Who had left it there and why? A burial hoard—loot hastily concealed? There were questions he longed to ask those about him concerning the other finds. Dared he try, without revealing to the curious that he knew more about this one than he had admitted?

If he was successful in keeping his find—then

was Tylos right? Could a deal be made with some
crewman? Only—how could he account for the
funds afterward? Well, there would be time, plenty
of time, to think that out later. It all depended on
how well he had hidden the tube, whether the tree
hollow would be safe.

Green and gold, red, blue—even colors he could
not put name to, shades melting into one another,
whirling, forming this design and that. Naill
longed to have it in his grasp again, just to hold
and watch for longer than the few moments he had
had it after freeing it from the ground. It was
beauty in itself—more than beauty: warmth. If he
could take it in his two hands, bring it to
Malani... Naill rolled over on the hard and narrow
bunk, his face to the unpeeled bark on the log wall.

"Out!" That was Kosburg's order as he banged
open the door. The tone of that bellow brought
instant obedience from his laborers.

Naill followed Hannosa into the open, to
discover the entire population of the garth was
assembled in the yard. A baby or two cried
protestingly in a mother's arms. Small children
stood sober-faced and wondering. Kosburg himself, cap in hand, was at the head of the family line
of Believers, facing a man wearing a long gray
cloak over the usual dull apparel of the settlers.

The stranger was bareheaded, and his shock of
uncovered hair and chest-spread of beard were as
gray as his cloak, so it was difficult to see where
fabric ended and hair began. Out of that forest of
beard a sharp beak of nose stuck, and curiously
pale red-rimmed eyes, one of which watered

constantly so that those involuntary tears drib-
bled into the waste of hair below, shone brightly.

"Sinners!" The cracked voice was, in its way, as
authoritative as Kosburg's.

A visible shiver ran along the line of Believers at
that accusation.

"The Dark One has chosen to set the snare of his
devising on this garth. Dark is only drawn to dark.
Your Sky has been clouded."

A moan came from some one of the women and
two of the children began to whimper. The cloaked
man lifted his head, turned his face to a sky which
was indeed cloudier than it had been that morning.
He began to chant words unintelligible to Naill,
the whole a croaking like the rasp of an ill-set saw.

Still looking skyward, the stranger pivoted his
body to the woodlands. And then, without watching his footing, he marched in heavy strides in that
direction. The Believers fell in behind him, men to
the fore, and Naill joined the laborers who brought
up the rear.

It was only coincidence, of course, but the clouds
continued to thicken overhead, the heat of the sun
was shut off, and from somehwere a chill breeze
had arisen. It wrapped about them as they came
into the clearing where lay the treasure cache.

Three times the Speaker marched about the
glittering heap on the ground. Then he took up the
ax that Lasja had earlier wielded and passed it to
Kosburg. The garthmaster reversed the tool,
bringing its heavy head rather than cutting blade
down on the objects there, battering and breaking
them into an undistinguishable mass of crushed

material, while the Speaker continued to chant. As Kosburg moved aside, the old man brought from beneath his cloak an old-model blaster.

Now he did look down as he aimed at the broken bits Kosburg had battered into shapelessness. The dazzling beam of the ray shot at that target, and the spectators pushed away from the heat of the blast. When the Speaker was done, there was only blackened earth in a pit. Whatever residue of metal had remained after that fiery attack had seeped into the ground itself. The Speaker turned to Kosburg.

"You will cleanse, you will atone, you will wait."

The garthmaster nodded his shaggy head. "We will cleanse, we will atone, we will wait."

They re-formed the procession and passed back across the fields to the homestead.

Tylos was the first to ask of the old hands, "Whatta they gonna do now?"

"One thing," Brinhold, another of the veteran laborers, told him. "We go to bed with flat bellies tonight. Lasja," he asked, "why didn't you just let that mess rot there? Why get the old man started on all this cleansin' business?"

"Yes!" There was a sullen chorus from his fellows. "Now we're gonna have to fast while they try to appease the Sky."

Lasja shrugged. "You know the Rule. Better go hungry a couple of days than have a full lesson-in'."

"He's right, you know," Hannosa pointed out. "It's just our bad luck we found it here. It's been about two years since Kosburg himself stumbled on that other one."

Naill looked up. "There was another found here, then?"

"Yes. Kosburg was out hunting his daughter. She was the strange one who used to go running off into the woods whenever she got free of the house. They said she wasn't right in the head." Hannosa's quiet face was shadowed by an expression Naill could not read. "Me, I'd say she was a reversion to what these people might have been before they became Believers. They used to have queer old tales on my world—a legend that there was an earlier race who had fled into the hills, gone into hiding, when invaders took over their land. And now and then the survivors of that earlier people would visit a house in which there was a newborn child and steal it away, leaving one of their own kind in its place."

"Why?" Naill asked. There was an odd feeling in him, another surge of that queer excitement that had tensed his body when he thought of the hidden tube.

"Who knows? Perhaps the blood was wearing thin and they had to have some of the new breed to mate with their own dying line. Anyway, the changeling—that was the name given to the child who was left—was alien and usually died young. Aillie was like that, unlike the rest of Kosburg's get—enough so in her ways to be of a different race."

"Yeah, she sure was different," Lasja agreed.

"Didn't have no luck neither."

"What happened to her?" Naill wanted to know.

"I told you about her—she took the Green Sick and they put her out in the forest like they always do. Only they needn't have made so big a to-do about her being a sinner! She never did no one no harm—only wanted to go her own way."

"But that is a sin here. In other places, too. No one must leave the herd—to be different is the complete and damning sin." Hannosa lay back on his bunk and closed his eyes. "Might as well relax and take it easy, boy. We don't work and we don't eat until the period of cleansing is past."

"How long?"

Hannosa smiled quietly. "That depends on how Kosburg intends to fee the Speaker. Old Hysander has quite a shrewd bargaining sense, and he knows that our worthy master wants to get those western fields cleared before the winter burning. There'll be some smart trading going on over that little matter just about now."

They had not found the tube; Naill hugged that thought to him as he lay through the hours of early evening. He had not seen it in that pile of objects destroyed. How soon dared he return to take it out of hiding? Good sense dictated a long wait for that. And yet his hands itched and twitched: he had a hunger for it as sharp as his hunger of body. Far back in his mind a small wonder stirred at this preoccupation with the alien artifact—why did it pull him so? Did it represent his chance of freedom, always providing he was able to get it to the port and make a deal with it? Or was it for itself that he wanted it so? And his wonder was tinged with a cat leap of fear.

Somehow Naill fought down that strong pull. He was physically tired, yet his mind was not lulled into any drowsiness. Instead he thought intently of small things—the leaves of the trees, the depths of the forest past the scars of the clearing, the aromatic smells, the way the wind lifted and rippled branch and bush.

He must have been asleep, for, when his eyes opened once again, it was dark. Naill stared into that dark. Overhead was the top bunk. He could hear the creak of wood, a sigh, a mumble where one of his roommates stirred unhappily. He was here, in Kosburg's garth—on a holding ripped out of Janus's forest covering by human will, hands, and stubborn determination.

But where had he been? Someplace else— someplace—right. Startled, Naill turned that impression over in his mind, tried to understand meaning through emotion. He had been else- where...that place had been right. He was here now—and it was wrong, wrong as a piece of machinery someone was trying to fit into a place where it did not belong, to do a job it could not manage.

It was hot. He was shut in, boxed, trapped. Naill moved softly, with sly pauses to listen, as an animal deep in the territory of a natural enemy might move. He wanted out—into the dark cool of the open. Then across the fields—to his tree—to what lay hidden there. His hands were shaking so much that he pressed them tight against his chest, and under them his heart beat wildly. Out—free—in the night!

His caution held until he was past the door of the bunkhouse. Then that wild exultation swept through him completely and he ran, seeming to skim across the rough surface of the field as if he were being drawn along by a tie uniting him to the waiting tree hollow. Dark here, but not the same kind of dark that had held back in the bunkhouse. Again that small part of his brain which could still wonder, was still unabsorbed by the desire that heated the rest of him, noted that he could *see* in this dark, that only the hearts of the deepest shadows were veiled to him.

And as he pushed into the roughly cleared land where they had been working, the wind wrapped around him softly, welcomingly. The leaves were not just set rustling by its fingers now; they sang—sang! And Naill wanted to sing, too. Only a last dying spark of caution choked that mutely in his throat.

Stench of burning.... He skirted the spot where the Speaker had used the blaster, not realizing that his lips were set in a snarl, that his eyes blazed, that he tasted anger, an anger out of all proportion to what had happened there only a few hours ago. Then he was through the veil of bushes, reaching up. His fingers on bark, smooth, welcoming bark....

Why welcoming? asked the now almost quiescent questioner in him, the questioner that vanished as his fingers passed from bark to tube. Naill held that out and gave a cry of pure delight.

Color—swimming color—shades combining, dancing—color from elsewhere, from the place where he was meant to be. A key . . . for the gate he must find—his own!

"Well, so that's it, boy. You did it—just like I kinda thought you did all along."

Naill spun around in a half crouch, the tube cupped in a hand tight against him. Tylos! Tylos standing there, grinning.

"Held out on 'em, Renfro? That was a right smart trick. Gonna pay off too—pay off for both of us."

"No!" Naill was only partly out of the spell that had held him since his awakening in the bunkhouse. The only decision he was certain of was that Tylos had no part, and would never have any part, of the thing he held.

"Now, you ain't gonna push me outta orbit, Renfro. All I gotta do is yell out nice and clear and you won't have no treasure left. You saw what they did to the rest of that today, didn't you?"

"If I don't have it, then you don't either." A portion of reasoning returned to Naill.

"True enough. Only I ain't gonna let you walk off with it neither. The boys back there, they said as how this is the second cache of this stuff found around here. Could be three, you know. And Sim Tylos, he's never been pushed outta no deal yet—not never by any Dipple creeper, he ain't. Give us a look."

The bole of the tree was hard at Naill's back. "No!"

"No?" Tylos's voice still held to the pitch of

ordinary conversation, but his hand moved. The light of the blue-green Janusan moon picked up the sheen of the knife blade, point up and out. "These here garthmen, they don't hold with blood-lettin'—not out and open—or so the boys say. Only I ain't no Believer—nor you neither. You give me that!" The knife sliced air. Tylos, armed with naked metal, avid for what Naill held, was not the same scrounging, sly, work-dodging weakling he had been.

"So!" Shadows out of shadow: Kosburg, his son, two more of his kinsmen, coming in a hunters' circle. "So—the evil still is—the sinning is yet! Well that we watched this night. Andon, you take the small one."

A loop of rope snapped out to pin Tylos's arms to his side, effectively halting before it began any struggle he might have made.

Kosburg regarded the small laborer. "He has not touched it. Intent but not yet the full sin. Put him in keeping. He shall be lessoned—well."

Another vicious jerk took Tylos off his feet, brought a hardly coherent stream of pleas and attempted self-justification out of him, until a kick from Andon impressed upon him the wisdom of silence.

"You—" Kosburg had turned to face Naill. "You are the complete sinner, infidel! You found—you concealed. You brought down upon us Sky wrath!"

His hand shot out and up with a speed Naill had not realized him capable of, and the club he held struck numbingly on Naill's forearm with force enough to bring a choked scream out of the younger man and throw him to his knees. Yet, in spite of his pain, he watched the tube, free of his grasp, roll to the open and lie there, warm, beautiful, glowing, in the moonlight. Only for an instant was it so. Then Kosburg leaped upon it, stamping with his heavy boots, grinding it into a powder that could not be told from the silvery wood dust—all that warmth and life.

Naill cried out, threw himself at the dancing hulk of the man treading in a frenzied shuffle up and down in the mass of withered leaves and churned earth. He did not see the blow that laid him limp and helpless a moment later.

Dark again, pain in his head and dark—a musty dark, the very taste of which made a sickness come into his throat. Dark.... Why should a fire be dark? And surely he lay in the heart of a fire from which he could not escape. The fire was in him, outside him—filled the world.

There was a long time when he awoke to the dark and the fire, to moan for water, to roll across an earth floor, tearing at his already tattered clothing, then to lapse once more into that other place, which he could never remember but which was so much more important than the dark and the fire.

Light struck in. It seared his eyes and made him cower and hold his hands before his face. He shrank away from the light, which mixed with the pain in his head and the fire that consumed him. But the light filled the world—there was no place to hide or shelter from it.

"Look at him!" Revulsion, fear—those emotions

reached him even in that place where he crouched trembling.

"Green Sick! Get him out of here—he has the Green Sick!"

Then the harsh croak of another voice. "The sinner is condemned by the Sky. Let him be dealt with after the custom, garthmaster."

Ropes coming at him, all around him, fastening to drag him out into the light, which was torture to his eyes. He was prodded, pulled, hustled along, sometimes wavering on his feet, sometimes falling to be dragged across the earth. This was a nightmare he could not understand, only endure, as might an animal on its way to the slaughter pen, hoping that it would not last long, that he could return once more to the dark.

Water—water running over rocks, downstream
under an open sky—water to drink, to pour over his
burning body. To lie in the midst of flowing
water....

Naill crawled on hands and knees, his eyes
narrowed slits against the terrible pain of light.
But there were spaces of cool shadows where the
light was muted, screened away, and those grew
larger and larger.

Iftcan.... The Larsh forces had attacked at
moonrise, and some weakling had let them seep
through the First Ring. So Iftcan had fallen, and

the Larsh now hunted fugitives from the Towers.

Naill crouched in the greenish shadow, his hands covering his face. Iftcan...Larsh. ...Dreams? Reality? Water—he must have water! Shivering he crawled on between trees, his hand groping, his legs sinking into a muck of decaying leaves and earth. Over him leaves whispered until he could almost understand a slurring, alien speech.

Now he could hear it, the murmur of water, and it grew to a roaring in his ears. He half fell, half rolled, down a slope to the side of a pool into which water was fed by a miniature falls he could have spanned with his two hands. A gasping rush plunged him into that water, where he laved hands, head, the whole upper part of his feverish body. He gulped from his cupped palms, felt the liquid run down his parched throat, wash about him, until at last he squirmed back—to lie limply, staring up into a lace of leaf and branch overhead, a round circle of open sky far above.

Naill ran his hands across his face, up over his head. There was a mat of stuff left between his fingers when he brought them unsteadily down to eye level again. Hair...loose, wet hair!

It took him a long moment to realize what he held, to raise his hand again for a more detailed examination of his head. The soaking at the pool had driven some of the bewilderment from his mind. He was Naill Renfro, off-world laborer on Janus. He had been sick...was sick.

Now he sat up abruptly, a cold shiver shaking him. Those searching fingers had encountered only bare skin, save one more small patch of hair, which had fallen from his scalp at first touch.

What—what had happened to him? Once more his hands went to his head, slipped across skin bare of hair, touched at the sides, stiffened at what they found there. He crouched, knees pulled to his chest, half bent over, breathing hard. Then his eyes, still squinted against the pain of light, saw a second pool, smaller, fed by the larger, but still of surface, a mirror in which the drooping foilage about it was reflected.

He crawled to that, leaned over so his head and shoulders would be reflected there.

"No!" that denial was torn out of him in a word half a moan. Naill drove his fist at the surface of the pool, to break that lying mirror, to blot out the thing it reported. But the ripples died away, and again he saw—not clearly, but enough.

Naill's hands went to his head for a second touch—exploration, to verify the reflection. Hairless head—ears larger than human, with the upper tips sharply pointed and rising well above the top line of his skull. And—he held his shaking hands out before him, forcing his eyes wide open for that study—his skin, which should have been an even brown, was now green! That was no fault of the tree shade, no trick of Janusan sunlight. It was true—he was green!

The tatters of his shirt were long since gone, and his bare chest, shoulders, ribs—all were green. He did not need to pull away the ragged breeches still belted about him, or kick off his scuffed and battered boots, to know that hue was universal.

What looked back at him from the pond mirror, what he could see with his eyes when he surveyed himself, was no longer human. He was Naill Renfro....

He was Ayyar....

Hands twisted, wrung, though he was unconscious of that despairing gesture. Ayyar of Iftcan, Lord of—of—Ky-Kye. The Larsh had broken the First Ring—they were into the Inner Planting. This was the time of the Gray Leaf and there would be no other seeding.

Naill swayed back and forth. He made no sound, but in him there was a wailing he could not voice. An ending—an ending—the time foretold had come upon them—the ending. For the barbarian Larsh had not the secret. They could destroy but they could not re-seed. When Iftcan fell, so did the Older Race die and the light of life and knowledge go out of the world.

But he was Naill Renfro! Iftcan—Ayyar-Ky-Kye—the Larsh. He shook his head, inched away from that mirror pool, tried to push out of his mind what he had seen there. He had a fever; he was simply delirious—that was it! His eyes—they hurt in the light, didn't they? They were playing tricks on him. That was it! It had to be!

Only now he no longer felt the burning heat consuming him. And he was hungry, very hungry. Slowly Naill got to his feet, found he could stand erect, walk. He stumbled along, scrambling up the small embankment down which splashed the miniature falls. There was a bush there, hung with puff-pods as big as his little finger. Mechanically he gathered them, popped them open with a snap, and eagerly stuffed the seeds they contained into his mouth. He had dealt with a full dozen of them before he began to wonder. How had he known they were edible? Also—when he opened them, why did he think he had done this many times before?

But of course he had. They were fussan, the hunters' friend, always to be counted upon at this time of the year, and he *had* feasted on them many times before. Naill paused, hurled that last pod from him as if its touch burned. He did not know about such things—he could not!

He collapsed on the ground again, quivering, his arms folded across his bent knees, his head forward on them, his body balled as if he wanted to pull back into nothingness, forgetfulness. Maybe if he slept once more, he would wake—truly wake. He slipped into the state he longed for. But when he lifted his head again, he was alert, his nostrils expanded, savoring, identifying scents, his ears picking up and naming the sources of sounds.

The hurtful sunlight was gone, the mist of twilight was balm to his eyes, and the soft shadows were no bar to seeing. Seeing! Naill could make out every rib of leaf, the network of veins across their surfaces—this was seeing such as he had never experienced before! Naill moved alertly, coming to his feet with a lithe readiness in what was almost one supple movement of muscles.

A borfund with cubs was feeding downstream. He did not need to see through the masking brush; his nose told him, and his ears picked up the crunch of double-toothed jaws moving greedily. And—aloft—there was a peecfren lying flat, belly to tree limb, watching him curiously. *Borfund— peecfren.* He repeated the names wonderingly in a low whisper. And his mind answered with mental pictures of living things he was sure he had never seen.

Then panic caught at him hard and heavy—as might the ray of a blaster. Blaster, that other part of him questioned—blaster? His hands flew to his head, clamping hard over those monstrous ears. *Borfund—blaster* ... memories alien to each other warring in his mind.

He was Naill Renfro—he was the son of a Free Trader, born in space ... Malani ... the Dipple ... Janus ... sale to Kosburg. Kosburg ... the garth: there was sanity. He must get away from here—back to where there were men ... men.

Naill broke away from the streamside, began to trot, weaving a way between the trunks of trees, trees that grew larger and larger as he moved away from the open glade of the stream. He went without path guidance but with purpose. Somewhere—somewhere there was an end to trees. It was open and in the open were men—men of his own kind. This was a fever dream and he must prove it so!

Yet as he went, nose, ears, eyes reported to his brain, and his brain produced answers to scent, hearing, sight, which were not a part of Naill Renfro at all. His headlong flight slackened as he leaned panting against a tree bole. As his panicky breathing began to slow, his head came up again and he battled shakiness, fear. The soft whisper of breeze in the leaves, the warmth—the caress of that same wind against his bare chest and arms.... And now that feeling of content, that this was right, the way life should be. As if he, too, reached down roots into the earth underfoot, raised swaying branch arms to the sky—a kinship with the forest world.

But he went on, though at a soberer pace, schooling his unease. He stopped once to strip long, narrow leaves from a low-hanging branch, crushed them between his palms, and then inhaled deeply of the scent from their bruised surfaces. He felt clear headed, alert, tireless, and eager.

However, that eagerness was replaced by another emotion as he came into the hacked trace of the settlers' war against the wild. Wilting leaves, broken branches—Naill's nostrils twitched in a spasm of distaste. He was scowling and unaware of it. The smell of death, decay, where it did not belong, and with it another stink—of an alien life form, defiling yet familiar.

He traced that smell out of the clearing, through the thinning of brush racked and torn by the logs pulled through it. Then he was on the edge of a field, a field where the butts of forest giants still stood as raw and ugly monuments to the death dealt them weeks ago. Naill snarled at the spoilation, and within him grew the disinclination to advance any farther into the open.

Pinpoints of light pricked beyond. His gaze centered there, narrowed. That was a garth—Kosburg's? Dared he chance moving closer? Yet he

must. He was a man . . . there were men. If he could
see them, speak with them, then he would know
that his eyes had deceived him back at the pool,
that he was not—not that thing!

Though that need drove him forward, Naill did
not go openly, nor did he realize that the action he
took, seemingly by instinct, would have been
totally foreign to Naill Renfro. His noiseless step—
with a foot planted with infinite care, his crouch-
ing run from one bit of cover to the next—was that
of a scout deep on a spying trip within the holdings
of the enemy.

Always that stink was heavy in his nostrils,
clogging up the air to sicken him, growing heavier
the closer he drew to the farmstead. He was still a
field away when the clamor broke out—the
hounds! Their baying was a war cry. Somehow he
knew—as well as if they had human speech and
shouted—that he was the quarry. So he had been
right in that long-ago guess: the garths kept those
four-footed hunters as a threat to laborer runa-
ways.

But Naill also remembered the custom at
Kosburg's. The animals had not been loosed in the
fields at night. There was too much chance of their
disappearing on some game hunt into the forest
and not returning. No, they patrolled inside the
wall of the garth yard.

And this was Kosburg's right enough. Naill
recognized the set of the big main house against
the night sky. There was a place where an active
man could climb the outer wall, look in at the top
floor window of that building, avoiding a descent

into the yard. Why he had this pressing need to do just that he could not have explained, but do it he must.

Though he flinched as the hounds bayed, he ran in a zigzag from shadow to shadow until his hands were on the stake wall near the house. He leaped, again not aware that his effort was far more powerful than any Naill Renfro could have made.

Killing trees to make shelters. Why did these people not know that trees could live and yet welcome indwellers? No—always this kind must kill, use dead things to pile about them until their lairs smelled—reeked of foul decay as did the pit of a hunting kalcrok!

The stench was almost more than he could bear, making his stomach protest. Yet he crouched before the incut which held an open window and looked into the lighted room beyond. He jerked and nearly lost his balance. That—that *thing*—two of them! They were monsters—as horrible as the smell of these dead lairs of theirs!

"Men" hammered one small part of his brain—or rather one man—the younger Kosburg—and a woman.

Monsters! The revulsion was sharp. Hairy as beasts—alien, not only in body but in mind. Looking at them now, Naill could in a way he could not understand savor their crooked thoughts, look into the narrowness of them. There was a wrongness every part of his own spirit rejected without pity.

The woman turned her head; her eyes by chance were on the window. Her mouth shaped into a

distorted square. She screamed tearingly, and
continued to scream with sharp, mindless cries.

Naill leaped outward, landing lightly on his
feet. Just as he had been revolted, had rejected
kinship with this species, so had the woman felt
about him. He ran, away from the stench of the
dead wood and the creatures who laired in it,
heading for the forest with its clean shelter.

But his repudiation of the garth was not the end.
An hour later he lay with heaving shoulders and
laboring lungs, hearing still the belling of the
hounds. They had brought them out, those
garthdwellers, to pick up his trail across the fields.
Only the fact that they had kept the dogs leashed
had saved him. But, judging from the sounds, they
had not ventured yet beyond the roughly cleared
land. Were they waiting there for daylight?

Then would the settlers overcome their dislike of
the forest and again put the hounds on his trail? Or
would he be safe if he retreated farther into the
deep woods? To go deeper, he would be lost to his
own kind—.... His own kind?

Spirit of Space—who were his kind now? Naill
shivered. His revulsion for the garth was a real
thing, as real as the heat of fever, the pain in his
head. He could not go to those people and claim
kinship—never again.

And that fact, standing stark and black in a
chaotic world, had to be faced. Something terrible
had happened to him—outside, inside. He was no
longer Naill Renfro. Though he was not now
looking at a strange reflection in a pool, he was

looking inside him at what had taken over his mind as well as his body.

Ayyar...who was Ayyar? If he were not Naill Renfro, then he was Ayyar. And he had to know who—what—was Ayyar, to whom the forest was truly home, to whom there came strange memories in ragged tatters. He must find Ayyar.

To do that...where did one search for such a weird trail? Physically, in the aisles of the forest; mentally, where? Because Naill did not know, he got to his feet and started in the only direction of which he was sure—back to the pool where he had first seen the mirrored face of someone who was no longer Naill Renfro.

Now that he had admitted that much, more and more of the new person took over. He stopped, pulled at the fastenings on the heavy boots that weighted down his feet. Footgear should be so different—made of borfund hide, fitting snugly, reaching from sole of foot to just below the knee— hunters' boots, through which one could feel any inequality of footing, not these clumsy coverings that locked the foot in prison, away from the good earth.

He pulled in irritation at his breeches. These, too—formless, coarse—were wrong. Green-gray silky stuff which caressed the body—spider thread wound and woven, packed in stass buds and the whole pressed firm to dry and age—that made proper clothing for the wood. Iftcan....But the Larsh were there. Naill stumbled against a tree, stood rubbing his head. Never a clear memory, just bits and patches...tiny fearsome scenes of men like himself, a desperate, driven handful, fighting among trees, trees in which they dwelt, going down one by one before a rabble horde of wild men...scattered, broken. Somehow he knew that had been the end of his kind.

His kind? What *was* his kind? Who was Ayyar? He blundered on, though he knew where he was going, that he would come out at the pool side.

And he did, falling down by that quiet pocket, drinking again from his cupped hands, slapping the pool's bounty over his sweating body. The rill ribboning from the smaller mirror pool, that should drain into the river—and beyond the river. He drew a ragged breath. Beyond the river stood Iftcan, tall and beautiful, silver leaves and singing leaves—the tower trees of Iftcan!

But he was tired, so very tired. As he relaxed beside the water, that tiredness caught at him. His feet hurt; perhaps he should not have thrown away those imprisoning coverings—only he could no longer stand their touch. Water rippled about his feet as he lowered them into the pool, soothing away smart and burn. He rubbed them dry with handfuls of grass and curled up drowsily.

The sound brought Naill out of sleep so deep dreams did not reach it. He lay where he was for a moment wrenched out of ordinary time, every part of him questioning by senses far more specialized than any off-worlder's. He rolled under a bush and brought his head around to look skyward.

No sun yet—but the lighter sky of dawn. Against it that blot—man-made. A flyer from the

port—small, two-man job—and coasting low. Naill
Renfro's memory supplied that much. But why—
how—?

Had Kosburg appealed for such help in his
hunting? Why? Trying to answer that was folly.
Soon it would be full day—and while Naill could
travel in the gloom of the forest, he dared not try to
face the open under the sun. Best move now: the
river—with across it Iftcan. Were the wild ones
still there? No, there was a dimness, a feeling that
what had happened in Iftcan was long past. But
that place drew Ayyar, and to its pull Naill Renfro
made no discouraging answer.

He started downstream, keeping under the roof
of the trees. Overhead he could follow the circling
of the flyer by the waxing and waning of the
engine purr. The pilot was hunting something
right enough, swinging the machine in a steady
pattern of rings over the forest. What he could see
below, save a carpet of tree crowns, puzzled Naill.
But the circling was too regular to doubt that the
port pilot did have a definite purpose, which could
only be one of search.

The rill that was Naill's guide joined another
stream, widened, developed a visible current.
Water things swam, or popped into the flood from
along the verge as he passed. He found another
fussan bush, stripped its pods and munched the
seeds as he went.

Then his nose warned danger—not the man
smell, no, this was vile in another way. His mind
supplied a murky picture of a danger that ran on
many legs, lurked, hid, pounced on anything

venturing into the forest strip it had appropriated as hunting territory. Naill leaped to catch at a low-hanging bough. Its elasticity helped to whip him up into the mass of the tree. And so he passed over that path with its evil smell, staying above and traveling from one tree limb to the next until the last taint of that odor was lost.

The day was on him, but the full dazzle of the sun did not reach here. Then he saw it blindingly bright before him, reflected from water, a sheet of swiftly running water. He shielded his eyes with his hands and tried to make out what lay on the opposite shore. Was there an Iftcan still?

Dark green, but only in patches. Elsewhere stands of white—stark white pillars, dead trees around which only small brush crept, a few stunted saplings grew. Yet in his mind it was alive! Silvergreen, tall and beautiful, the tree towers of Iftcan! If he could only remember clearly—and more.

Naill cupped hands over his eyes, peering through finger slits to shut out the light as much as he could. The river was wide, but there were rocks jutting above its shrunken summer surface. One could cross by aid of those. Only—it was open sky there and he could hear the hum of the flyer.

Suppose—suppose a man could slip down into the flood a little to the east, let the current carry him in an angle downstream to where a point of tumbled rocks speared into the water? A mat of old storm flotsam clung and banked there to form cover. Beyond it was brush into which one could duck.

Naill tensed, listening to the sound of the overhead menace, trying to gauge just how far away it was, speculating as to how much of the riverbank its pilot could observe. He dared not look aloft into the sky; his eyes protested even this amount of sunlight and he feared blindness.

He dropped his hands and eased off his breeches. Green body against the earth might have a better chance. Now...! As well as Naill could judge, the flyer was on the farthest edge of the loop it was traveling. He began his crawl downslope to the water, keeping to all the cover there was. The flyer was headed back!

Naill froze, hugging the earth, feeling the despair of an insect overhung by a giant boot ready to stamp it flat. He found himself furiously willing blindness on the pilot, invisibility for himself.

The motor beat loudly in his ears. Was the machine hovering on repel ray right over him? By a gigantic effort of will he lay quiet, made himself wait and listen.

No, not a hover—it was passing! Passing south. When it reached the far point of the swing, he could make a run that should slip him into the water. He listened—then moved.

The water was cold; it chilled his bare body as he tried to enter without betraying splashes. Then he let the current pull him along. Above the sound of the water he caught the hum of the flyer on its backsweep.

Naill's nails grated on a rock as he clung in its shadow, trying to make himself small. Luck was with him—the machine was passing over. He loosened that frantic hold, allowed himself to drift downstream. When he caught against the rock point, he could control himself no longer but scrambled out of the water, scuttled over the rocks, and dived into brush cover at the foot of one of those bleached bones—the dead tree towers of Iftcan.

For several long moments he merely lay there, listening, fearing that he had betrayed himself in that small burst of panic. Only the hum was fading again; the flyer was going north. He had made the crossing undetected.

Now to find a hiding place in which to wait out the day, to favor his smarting eyes. Naill put out a hand, drew it down the dry bark of the dead tree against which he had taken refuge. It was huge, this tall trunk. Was this not Iftcan, whose trees had known a thousand planet years of carefully tended growth?

His hand fell away as he drew back from the dead. In its way he knew a little of the same revulsion he had known at the garth. Living things did not shelter among the dead.

Naill moved on from the verge of the river, keeping prudently under cover. Always about him were the leafless trees, long since finished, yet standing as monuments to their own ends.

They were quiet, those forest aisles of Iftcan. His passing alerted no bird or small living thing; no insect sped away. And here no breeze sang a song he could almost but not quite put words to. At least the flyer had not followed; it still circled above the river.

Naill was through the First Ring now. Here was a belt of denser green, and in it lifted the crowns of two saplings, untended, unshaped—yet the species was not dead, then! Naill pushed his way to one, regardless of scratches and the stinging whip of small branches, to stand and run his hand along its trunk. It seemed that the bark pulsed under his palm as if he stroked a pet animal that responded by arching its body to fit closer into his hand.

> "Far, far, and first the seed,
>   Then the seedling,
>   From the rooting, to the growing.
>   Breath of body, stir of leaf,
>   Ift to tree, tree to Ift!"

He crooned the words hardly above a whisper. What did they mean, demanded Naill Renfro. Growing words, power words, words of recognition, replied Ayyar. The death was not wholly death! The triumph of the Larsh was not complete. And these saplings had seeded aright—somewhere one or more of the Great Crowns was yet alive!

Weaving a path between the dead, he cut deeper

into the unknown. Another living sapling! And
then...

He stared in wonder. Old, very
old...huge....This—his tangled memory sought,
found—this was Iftsiga! The ancient citadel of the
south. And it lived!

No ladder hung from the great forelimb stretching high above his head. There was no way to
reach the hollow he could sight where that mighty
limb joined the parent trunk. And he had no wings
to whisk him aloft. Naill's head turned slowly as
he caught, on the breeze ruffling the tree leaves,
the slight hint of another scent.

Tracing it, he found what otherwise he might
have overlooked—the sapling ladder carefully
hidden in the leaf mat on the ground. To off-
worlder or settler it would have been nothing more
than a dead tree with stumps of branches still
sprouting jaggedly from its trunk. Ayyar of the
Iftin knew it instantly, swung it up against the
bulk of Iftsiga, and climbed it nimbly to a limb
that was wide enough to accommodate four of his
kind walking abreast.

He traveled along it and paused for only a
moment at the hollow of the doorway before
stepping into the past—the far, far past.

The walls of that circular room were very thick,
as they should be when the sap and life of Iftsiga
were housed within them, a living shell to encase
the hollowed center. The odor that had guided him
to the ladder was stronger here. Yet the upper room
was empty.

Light pulsed on the ceiling over his head—

lorgas, the larvae that clustered in the tree cores, attracting to them by that phosphorescence of their bodies the minute flying creatures on which they fed. They made a ring about the opening that held the stair pole reaching up—and down—in the middle of the tree. And Naill's present interest was downward.

He fitted his hands and feet into the old slots in the pole and descended nimbly. The odor of occupation was still here, but it had been three or four days since those others had left.

Another room—but not an empty one. Naill swung away from the stair well to look about him. The subdued light given off by a second cluster of lorgas was satisfactory. Carven stools—several. A neatly piled collection of sleep mats. And—against the far wall...

He made for that, his hands reaching out eagerly to lift the inlaid cover of a chest that was a masterpiece of construction, an intricate combination of many kinds of wood. Naill went down on one knee to roll back the protecting bark cloth. Then his breath expelled in a hiss of pleasure and content as he picked one of the exposed weapons from its oily nest of floosedown.

It caught the soft light, glinting green-silver. And it might have been forged for him alone, that sword with the leaf-shaped blade and the perfect balance, so well did its gemmed hilt fit to his hand as he swung it experimentally. To Naill Renfro it was a strange, if beautiful, weapon; to Ayyar it was comfort, an answer to his desires for defense.

A sword, even completed with scabbard and

shoulder belt, as this was when he explored the contents of the arms chest further, was not all he needed. Clothing, food, shelter.... He began to examine the other furnishings of the tree room.

Clothing—packed carefully in a long basket of woven splints with dried, aromatic leaves to be shaken from the folds as he pulled it forth to measure against his own lank body. He stood up minutes later, the soft green-silver-brown fabric stretching and accommodating itself to every movement of his frame, in tight breeches, a tunic laced over the chest with a silver cord, the supple boots he had longed for earlier. Also he wore a cloak with a hood, and a gemmed buckle to fasten at the throat—all strange and yet very familiar.

Naill smoothed the fabric across his thighs. He had given up wondering why he knew what he knew...all the bits about this other life. He welcomed Ayyar and Ayyar's broken memories, his alien knowledge, instead of striving to thrust that odd intruder out of his mind. This was Ayyar's world—now his. Wisdom dictated that he accept that fact and build what future he could upon it.

He sat down on the pile of mats, munching a crumbling cake of stuff Ayyar had welcomed eagerly, and tried to put his thoughts in order, to reach back to the beginning of all this. Naill Renfro had found a cache of the mysterious treasure that turned up without reason here and there on the holdings of the Believers. And from that had come all the rest.

The Green Sick—he could remember that

dimly—of being dragged out of Kosburg's prison
room and hearing his fate pronounced: exile and
death alone in the forest. But Naill Renfro had not
died—not wholly; he had instead become Ayyar of
the Iftin, who also could remember—a battle
through a city of towering trees and the bitterness
of an overwhelming and complete defeat.

And physically he was no longer Naill Renfro
either. He was a green-skinned, big-eared forest
dweller who apparently could frighten garthmen
into a panic...a monster.

Green Sick—change—monster.... The procession of events made sense of a kind. But there had
been others who had fallen ill in the past—had
they all been changed? His hands paused with the
bread stuff. If so, then they could be out here, too.
They could be the ones who had left their scent,
their signs of occupation, here—right where he
was! He would not be alone in his exile!

They had been here, and left their possessions
laid up carefully against a future return. To wait
here for them—that might well be his brightest
move. At any rate he needed rest, and he wanted to
do nothing to provoke any investigation from
those who rode the flyer. He would wait until
night...for the night was his!

Naill finished the bread, flicked the crumbs
from his fingers and lay back on the mats, pulling
the cloak over him, his unsheathed sword beside
him where hand could reach and curl about its hilt
in an instant. He blinked drowsily at the ring of
lorgas. Some had spun threads beaded with sticky
dots to better entrap their lawful prey, and those

drifted lazily in the air. The quiet held him and then it seemed as if the living tree that encased this chamber exerted its own soothing spell, and he slept, this time with no dreams at all.

How long he slept Naill could not have told, but he awoke quickly, with every faculty alert. The chamber was as it had been; he could hear no sound. Sitting up, he stretched, got to his feet, and went to the pole ladder. On impulse he descended another level in Iftsiga.

Here was a third circular chamber, slightly larger. There were chests against the walls, one pulled away from the rest. Naill went over, lifted the lid. He ruffled aside more bark cloth packing, only to be startled into an exclamation.

Green-stoned necklace, box, tube of glowing colors—piece by piece he beheld an exact duplicate of the treasure he had uncovered in the clearing! Naill lifted out the color tube. It was the same as the one Kosburg had stamped into the dust, in every flit of color, change of pattern, along its surface! But why? Slowly he took out each object and studied it carefully before putting it aside for the next. The chest was still far from empty; there was a second layer of cloth—and then another treasure set!

With the same care as he had brought them out, Naill repacked the objects. He sat on the floor, his hands still resting on the lid of the chest as he thought this through. Two sets of treasure, perfect reproductions of each other—and both like the set he had seen destroyed at Kosburg's. He wished he knew if all the other treasure caches the settlers had blasted had also been as these. If so—why?

Ritual objects placed as offerings or to mark graves? Naill tried to find the answer in Ayyar-memory, but there was no response from his new alter ego. Either Ayyar had known nothing of such things, or else there was a block between his memory and Naill Renfro. But there had to be a purpose for the caches—in the forest and in storage here. This chest had been moved out of line. Why? To better abstract part of its contents recently?

Why? Naill could have screamed that aloud in his frustration.

Perhaps somewhere else in Iftsiga he could find his answers. But when he went back to the pole ladder, he discovered that the opening to the chambers below was sealed. And for all his exasperated pounding, that round of wood did not give way. Baffled, he climbed once more into the room where he had slept and then decided to go up.

The dim light of twilight came in through the limb door as he reached the entrance chamber. There was no sound from without, save the rustle of leaves. After a moment or two he climbed to the level above. Here were no lorgas on the ceiling, only gray outer light admitted through window holes. The chamber was empty save for powdery dust and the ghostly remnants of long-shed leaves. Perhaps every upper level was the same, but he decided to try one or two more.

Naill was still on the pole ladder when he heard it—a furious snapping, ending in a hooting call, low pitched, yet with an urgency in it that could

not be denied. And the Ayyar part of him
responded to that with a burst of speed. He
scrambled through the ladder well to face fluttering, beating wings, to look into a feathered face
where great eyes were ringed darkly to seem the
larger. And when that set gaze met his own, Naill
was again startled.

Speech? No—the hoots and clicks of the big
curved bill did not add up to human speech. Yet
this flying thing recognized him, welcomed his
aid, traded on an alliance between them! Not an
alliance such as existed between man and animal
as he had known, but between one species of
intelligent life form and another of equal if
different mentality. It was as shocking in that first
moment of realization as if the tree holding them
both had broken into intelligible words.

The bird thing was hurt. It had been blasted
by—by men! Naill had an oddly distorted mental
picture of hunters, which must have flashed from
the other's mind to his. Someone from the port,
trying to relieve the tedium of a planet-side stay,
had gone hunting.

A wing was trailed for his inspection, showing
singed feathers, the raw bite of a blaster burn. It
was big, this Janusan bird—with a wing spread of
close to five Terran feet, its body, puffed in fluffy
white-gray feathers, standing on huge talons
intended for hunting. Now its demand for aid and
attention grew sharper in his head.

It allowed him to inspect the burn. The wound
was not bad enough to incapacitate it entirely.
Naill received another blurred mental impression

of the victim fluttering from tree to tree, working
its way farther into the forest and away from the
off-world invaders. But he had not the slightest
idea in the world of what to do for the injury.

The bird squatted down before him as he sat
cross-legged. It folded its good wing to the body,
kept the other outspread. And Naill winced as that
strange mind deliberately invaded his own. It was
as if one had two recordings, similar in most major
features, differing in smaller details, which must
be fitted one upon the other for a matching of
patterns. That could not be done entirely—but on
the major points where the match could be made ...

"Yes!" Naill said as if the bird could understand.
"Yes!"

He swung down the pole ladder to the room that
had been inhabited. The same woven wicker
basket that had held the clothing had what he
sought, a pouch he had overlooked. With its cord
hooked over his arm, Naill reclimbed to where the
bird waited.

Awkwardly he mixed powdered leaves from one
small box into a paste held by another, then spread
that dressing with all the care he knew onto the
raw burn. When he had done, the bird hooted again
and walked about in a circle as if testing its ability
to do that, though it did not try its wing.

"Who—what—are you?" Naill asked suddenly.
But Ayyar was answering that for him.

A quarrin, the tree dwellers who far in the past
had made a pact and alliance with the Iftin, who
were also tree dwellers and lovers of the forest
world. Hunter on two legs, hunter on two wings,

warrior armed with sword, warrior armed with talons and sundering hooked bill, they had hunted, they had fought side by side when need arose, because by some trick of nature they had been able to communicate after a fashion. It was not an alliance between thinking man and instinct-ruled animal or bird, but a partnership between two species of equal if different prowess. Hurt, the quarrin had returned to the place where it could expect aid, and it claimed that from Naill as a right.

Now, moved by something he could not understand, Naill held out his right hand. The round head, with its upstanding ear tufts of feathers—not too unlike his own pointed ears—leaned forward a little.

The big eyes, with the yellow-red fires deep in them, studied his outheld hand with odd intentness. Then the head bent more, the cruelly hooked bill opened and closed on his flesh, not to rend or tear, but in firm pressure, as a man's hand might clasp his fellow's hand in a signal of greeting and friendship—a quick grasp, over almost at once. But Naill smiled slowly. Naill-Ayyar was no longer alone in Iftcan the Dead.

"Hoorurr,"—Naill had made of the bird's call a name—"I don't think they *are* coming again—soon." He sat in the upper door to Iftsiga, a perch he had made his own for hours at a time while he waited for the unknown to return.

Three days—or rather nights, for the nights were now his time of action—and no sign that any Ift had climbed that ladder or made camp within the tree bole for years. Yet Naill's nose had told him that he had arrived there only hours after them that first day.

In spite of patient mental probing and attempts

to communicate with the quarrin, he could not
learn whether or not the bird had been left behind
by any of his kind, or if the relation between the
winged tree dweller and the footed ones had been
more than a casual one of simple acquaintance.
With no speech in common, the mental contact
could convey only imperative ideas and needs.

But Hoorurr was company and Naill fell into the
habit of talking to the bird. There was no reason to
remain in Iftsiga if it was now deserted. And who
had been those temporary indwellers? Other
changelings such as himself—or remnants of the
true Iftin who had survived, broken shadows of
what they had once been?

The trouble was that Ayyar's knowledge still
reached Naill only in bits and pieces, and most
often widely separated and disconnected bits and
pieces. Matters pertaining to the daily round of
maintaining life—that information came to Naill
easily. He had known just where to go within the
tree to tap the water supply; he knew food supplies
and how to seek them out. But all the rest—these
strange memories were hazy, impossible to fit
together.

Once on Janus there had been two peoples—the
Iftin dwelling in trees, possessing knowledge that
allowed them to shape and tend growing things so
that they had a kinship of feeling, if not of blood
and body, with the forest; and the Larsh, more
primitive, not resembling the forest men either
mentally or physically, fearing the "magic" of the
tree peoples, dreading it enough to want to kill—to

stamp it out—as the garthmen fought to eradicate
the forest nowadays.

The Larsh were not off-world settlers, though.
And the war between Iftin and Larsh had been
centuries ago. Iftin had been dead a long, long
time. Then why did Ayyar remember? And how
had Ayyar become in part Naill Renfro—or Renfro
Ayyar?

Whenever his thoughts poured into that familiar path, Naill was uneasy, sometimes treading
around the tree chambers while Hoorurr clicked
his bill impatiently.

"No," Naill repeated now, "they are not returning. All was stored here for a period of waiting.
Those swords were in oiled covering, the rest was
put away. They have gone—so I go after!"

If he could pick up the trail of those who had
been here, find them, then he would know the
truth! And there had been no sign that either
settlers or port flyer had ventured this side of the
river. He had never heard of Iftcan at the garth.
Yet such a forest space with the trees already dead
would have been seized upon by the settlers had
they known of it. But was he too late in trying to
trace the unknowns?

"Hoorurr"—he looked straight into the bird's
big eyes—"this I must do—go after them." With
his mind as well as his lips, Naill strove to make
his need plain, experiencing once more that weird
mix-match of thought pattern.

The bird stretched wide wings, moved the
injured one experimentally, and then sounded its
haunting call. Hoorurr would manage, but Naill

must walk this path alone; the quarrin did not intend to leave Iftcan and its chosen hunting grounds.

It was one thing to come to such a decision, another to carry it out. Naill, down from Iftsiga, the sapling ladder once more concealed as he had first found it, stood in the shadows, the difficulty of his quest brought forcibly home to him as he looked around. He did not believe that he would find those he sought still within the bounds of Iftcan, even if others of the tree towers still lived.

But now—north, south, west—which way? South were the spreading garths. He thought he could safely rule out that direction. And to the northeast was the spaceport, eastward more garths. Somehow he believed he would not discover those he sought too near any off-world place. West, where the maps said one of the narrow fingers of sea lay?

In the end he decided to let his path be set by chance—and the wind. For the wind sighing through the leaves was oddly company of a sort, a comforting voice overhead—and the wind pushed him west. He had made his first mistake in lingering so long at Iftsiga; the trace of scent which might have guided him must now be lost. Yet he still depended upon his nose to pick up hints of life in the dead forest.

Life there was—Ayyar memory identified most of it—animals, flying things, in the patches of vegetation that straggled among the bone-bare boles of the dead tree towers—more as he came to the First Ring.

Here the trees were scorched with ancient fire, eaten away as they lay toppled to the ground. And the spreading wasteland was dreary but already half covered once again by a ragged growth of rank things, things that the Iftin would neither encourage nor allow to root near their city in the old days. Naill's half knowledge took him on detours to avoid certain plants from which came a stench to twist the nostrils. And there were thorn-studded vines running lines to entrap unwary feet.

In that unwholesome mass lurked other life inimical to his species. This was a waste where Larsh destruction had begun a work of defilement, and the evil that had always waited for a chance to break the defense wall had entered in greedily, to take possession of the once clean city. The inner part of Iftcan had become a sad place; this was a filthy charnel house, and Naill hesitated to force a path in that direction. As he stood there, Ayyar memory stirred, supplied a strange emotion. He felt more than disgust... danger... a barely understood warning that something old and perilous lay there.

There remained the river. To travel along its bank should eventually bring him to the sea. Why the sea? The forest was Iftin country—not that restless water to the west. Yet... the wind blew him seaward.

Naill cut away from the edge of the waste to the running water, reaching the river, he believed, not far from the point where he had swum to safety. The moon made a silver ribbon, waved and broken by the current, to serve as his trail marker.

When dawn showed gray, he made himself a
nest in a thicket well shaded from the sun, and lay
there, lulled by the water's murmur. In that half-
drowsing state, another scrap of Ayyar memory
made for him a vivid picture of a boat—oared by
men who wore the Iftin dress, watched shadows
with Iftin eyes, bore Iftin swords—steered down
between threatening rocks where water boiled, a
boat, bearing Iftin warriors to the sea. This was an
old trail, then, this water one.

Naill was on the trail again in the late evening
when he found the camp site, coming down into a
rock-enclosed hollow to stand, nostrils expanding,
picking up that lingering trace of scent that the
wind had not pushed away. He went down on his
knees, studying the floor of the hollow, trying to
pick out some track that would prove his guess
correct.

River sand filled that stone-walled cup, and he
sifted the coarse stuff through his fingers, until he
uncovered a fussan pod, split open, seed gone. A
pod here with no bush nearby to shed it
naturally—he was right! This was the path of
those he sought. As had the boatmen of his
memory, they were heading seaward!

His pace became a trot when he left that camp;
he was ridden by an increasing feeling of urgency,
that he must catch up with the strangers, reach
them soon, or it would be too late. Too late? Why?
Just another of the many mysteries that had been
his portion on Janus.

But Naill could not throw off that feeling, and it
became so strong that he did not pause with the

dawn, but kept on, trying to travel under cover. By mid-morning he was forced to admit he could not go any farther. For the forest was dwindling. Since early light the larger trees, standing fewer and farther apart, had vanished altogether. Now smaller growth and bush were common, with wide strips of grass open between them.

Naill found shelter in a shade that was neither constant nor thick enough to make him truly comfortable. His head pillowed on his arm, his body and legs aching with fatigue, he tried to rest. But that need for speed ate at him, so this time was only one of impatient waiting for the dusk.

In the twilight he went on into the open, to top a hill there and walk into a change of wind. Now the breeze was chill, salt-laden. Beyond lay ridges of smaller hills, some half sand masses. And ahead of those were curling feathers of white marking waves along a strand.

Immediately before Naill was a low scoop of land where the river emptied into the ocean. Cliffs raised walls on either hand. Naill looked to them and his hand came to his mouth.

Light! A spark of light! He could not have been mistaken—surely he could not! And why such a beacon there? A signal? Or some off-world explorers' encampment? Prudence dictated caution to temper his first wild desire to run toward that light. He waited in suspense, but there was no second spark there. Had he been mistaken, seeing what he had hoped to see?

Best go there and be sure. Naill started down the rise, slipping and sliding through the loose earth, heading for the northern cliff point. Distances must have been deceiving, or else the tricky footing in the sand hills slowed his progress. He had no way of measuring time, but he thought that at least an hour had passed and he had yet to reach the foot of the cliff where the spark had blazed. He could smell the sea in the wind, hear the pound of the waves along the shore. Otherwise he might be plodding through an empty and deserted world.

Here was the cliff. Surveying its rugged wall, Naill sighted nothing except the rock. But that offered hand holds and toe openings, and he could climb, reach the crown, make sure.

Naill pulled himself up and over, sprawled panting. He had been right! They had been here, those from Iftcan, or some like them, and a very short time ago. He rolled over on his side, too spent for the moment to rise, and saw a hollow in a pinnacle of rock that made a pointed, easily detected finger in the night sky. And in that hollow...!

On hands and knees he came to it, thrust his hand out to explore a plate of stone. On it were ashes yet warm enough to make him jerk back his fingers. A signal surely.... Set why? For whom?

The reason must lie still beyond. Naill clung to the rock and wriggled out to the very edge of the northern drop. Again he looked down into a sea basin. The cliff on which he was had a twin perhaps half a mile away, and between them the waves washed well inland, making a natural and protected harbor. A harbor which now sheltered...

A ship?

But that object was unlike any ship Naill had ever seen. He would rather have thought it a log, one of the gigantic logs from the old forest, bobbing up and down in the hold of the waves. There were no oars, no sails, no break in the rounded surface lying above the waterline. And this time Ayyar memory did not supply him with an explanation.

Yet he knew that that huge log did not ride in the waves without purpose. Did it hold men, men such as himself, as the tree houses of Iftcan had held and sheltered? And if so, where would it carry them now?

There was no sign of any movement, except the slow swing of the log in the waves. That signal. ...Naill studied the drop below him, seeking a path to the water's edge. But he was forced to retreat some distance inland before he found a ledge leading to a zigzag cutting, which revealed the fact that visits to the signal post on the cliff must be regularly made. He rounded a last outshoot pinnacle and met a faint path leading to the beach.

That log, which had apparently floated without control or direction when he had watched from the cliff, was now turned end on toward the sea and was traveling out, against the toss of waves, as if below the water surface some propelling agent moved.

"No!" Naill cried that aloud, ran stumbling through the sand to the water's edge, where a wave foamed about his ankles. There was nothing to be seen save the log. And that was moving with a purpose, under command, he did not doubt. It was already passing between the outer hooks of the cliffs, fast turning into only a black blot on the water.

Too late—he had come too late!

Slowly he retreated out of the wash of the foam, and it was then that he saw those other marks, indentations one could not truly call footprints, a cluster of them where the sand had been widely disturbed... the embarkation point?

Since the tracks were all that remained, he studied them. They marked, he believed, the end of a fairly well-defined trail leading back into the interior of the continent. One source of answer to his collection of mysteries, the log—which was more than a log—was now beyond his pursuit. But this trail, did it lead from Iftcan? Or from some other and more enlightening beginning? It was recent, made within hours, and it was the only trace the strangers had left him.

Naill turned his back on the sea, where the log was now only a black point, and began to walk along the trail of those who had manned that queer vessel.

Much later he lay on a mat of leaves against the trunk of a tree, peering through a screen of brush at what he had least expected to discover at the end of the trail he had traced, through two nights, well away from the seashore, across the river again, and southward into the settlers' Fringe lands. During the past hour he had been skirting the ragged edges of a garth—not Kosburg's, too far west for that, and it was smaller, a newer beginning for some less well-established settler.

The strangers he scouted after had come here from the northeast—perhaps straight from Iftcan. And they had spent some time slipping in and around the outer edges of the clearing to the south and west, as if they were on the hunt for something—or someone. He had discovered one place where at least two encamped for some time— perhaps through a day or more. Had they been spying on the activity about the garth? Planning a raid? They had certainly taken every precaution to keep their presence a secret.

Now he had come to the focal point of their explorations. They had scouted, they had spied, and then they had finished here—finished what? Naill only knew that from this place led the return trail to the seashore. So here their mission had been either accomplished or abandoned.

It was early morning, leaving him very little time to make his own search before having to retire to the tree hollow where those others had waited out the sunlight hours before him. He could hear the sounds of awakening life at the garth several fields' lengths away—the howl of a hound, the chittering complaint of a phas disturbed against its will. If the garthmaster was a pusher, his field laborers might be hurried out before dawn to start their day's work here.

There was one glimmering of an idea that had ridden Naill for the past half hour. He had begun to believe that what he sought here was buried: a cache set skillfully and with cunning to be discovered by someone from the garth, treasure trove—not remaining hidden from vanished years in the past, but from days earlier. And if his guess was the truth, he believed he knew now where to look for its confirmation.

He scrambled around a log, began a careful search of the ground. But what he sought was not located near the fallen trees waiting to be branch-stripped and hauled away. It had been placed in the midst of a tangle of wild berry bushes. The swollen, yellow fruited brambles had been carefully rearranged to hide turned earth, but there was a gleam of metal artfully exposed to catch the eye there.

And the berries—Naill recognized those, too. They were sweet, entrancing to anyone who was thirsty. The bait was excellently planned. Any man working here would be drawn to strip a handful of the fruit during a rest period, perhaps to pick more to share with his fellows, pick enough to uncover that piece of metal, and then...

Naill twitched the bramble back into place. A call from the garth moved him to haste in his withdrawal. He had been right; they were already heading for clearing work, early as it was. And if they brought hounds with them...!

He slipped among the bushes and ran, hoping that the workers were not accompanied by dogs, believing he could outwit any settler who tried heavy-footedly to follow his trail. Minutes later he was at the hiding place the trappers had established, listening intently to the growing noise of a phas-drawn roller bumping over the fields in the direction of the clearing, near which the bramble hung.

Trappers—he was certain of that now—trappers who had left a baited trap! He had been caught in such a trap. Now he was able to fit one more piece into his broken picture. The tube he had hidden, held, wanted for his own—and the Green Sick. Was one born of the other? That could be. Those who sinned by concealing or handling the treasure were punished speedily for that sin—cause and effect, which was closer to the truth than the settlers knew for sure.

But the purpose of this elaborate scheme still eluded him. By some alien means—and Naill was now certain his illness was no natural ailment, unless it could be a Janusan disease induced and controlled by will—he had become a different person, strange to his former self, not only physically but mentally, too.

Traps—trappers—the log ship—Iftcan—Ayyar. . . . Naill's head ached dully. It was as if inside his skull there was a stirring, a battering against some tightly bolted door . . . some hidden part of him fighting for freedom. He caught the reek of man scent, of animal odor. But there was no tonguing from a hound. For the period of the day he must keep under cover.

As much as his senses flinched from the alien activities of the garth, Naill knew that he would remain—if not in this special hideout, then nearby—until he witnessed the springing of the trap, learned what did follow its discovery.

EIGHT

THE TRAPPED

His hiding place, Naill speedily discovered, had been carefully chosen by those who had first used it as an observation post. It gave him a good view of the clearing. The working party that came there now was smaller than those Kosburg had mustered. There were only two slave laborers, and three bearded Believers, one of those hardly more than a boy, his beard a few silky straggles on his chin.

They began work well away from the brambles that masked the trap, and the garthmaster kept them busy with a vigor and concentration that suggested he ruled the holding with an iron-rooted will. The labor of clearing was the same Naill had sweated over, but inside him now a new anger coiled and raised. This destruction of what was right and good to make more ugly bareness! He realized his fingers had curved about the hilt of that leaf-bladed sword, that he was eying hotly the leader of that work gang.

To remain where he was could be the rankest folly, and yet he was held there by that curiosity, the need for knowing what would happen if and when the treasure was found. Would one of those laborers uncover the cache out of sight of his master and seek to conceal part of it for his own?

Naill was so intent upon watching the workers that he missed the arrival of a second small group at the edge of the clearing. And he was startled to see suddenly the flap of a skirt.

His first impression of the womenfolk of the Believers had been that they courted dour plainness with the assiduity with which off-world women strove to develop the current ideal of beauty. Their sacklike clothing, fashioned of the same dull browns, shabby grays, and sullen black-greens the men also wore, carefully concealed any hint of form, while their hair was screwed back into tightly netted knots. Away from their own hearthsides they followed the dictates of the Rule and went masked, a strip of cloth with holes for eyes, nose, and mouth rendering them both anonymous and safely hideous.

Not that they ever ventured very far from the buildings of the garth. In all the time Naill had been at Kosburg's, he had never seen any of the women farther afield than the stableyard, except driving, fully masked and covered with additional muffling cloaks and hoods, to the weekly Sky Stand of the elect.

But here a woman escorted three smaller figures, all masked. Baskets on arm, they were heading toward the berry-hung bushes.

"Ho!" The garthmaster upped his ax for a swing, to drop it without delivering the full blow. He was no giant to match Kosburg, but a thin, active man, and the forward-thrusting beard he displayed was fair and lank.

The woman stopped, turned to face him, her smaller companions retreating a little behind her as if cowed by such public notice of their being. They remained so while the garthmaster climbed a fallen tree trunk and came to them.

"What do you do here, girl?" he demanded.

One work-reddened hand gestured at the heavy harvest of berries.

"These will be uprooted soon." Her voice was low, without expression. "There is no need to waste this present crop."

The garthmaster considered that point, approached the berry bushes closer as if to estimate the value of their wild abundance. Then he nodded.

"Keep to your work, girl," he ordered. "And make haste—we want to clear here before night."

The children scuttled to the picking as he strode away. But for a moment the woman stood where she was, her head now turned to the forest, her eyes, Naill thought, not on the berries at all but on the woodland behind them. Then he saw her do an odd thing—put out her hand and draw one finger down the graceful bend of a stem from which hung a cluster of small white flowers. Her head turned sharply right and left, and then she bent to smell that flowering spray before she went on to strip the berries into her basket in quick, efficient motions.

Whether by chance or design, she pushed her way, picking as she went, until the patch of bramble was a screen between her and the other working party. Then, having added a last handful of fruit to her basket, she set it carefully on the ground and straightened to her full height, once again facing the depths of the forest.

Her hands went to the back of her hood, fumbled with the cords, and she jerked off her mask with an impatient gesture. Her head was up, her chin raised, with a movement into which Naill read defiance.

She had the pallid skin of all garthside women, and her features held no hint of beauty. But she was young, no more than a girl. A high-bridged nose centered above a small mouth, one with thin, pale pink lips. Her eyes were well set, but above them were thick brushes of brows, giving them a harsh and forbidding half frame. No—she was not even remotely pretty by off-world standards, and that alien which was within Naill now found her pale skin repulsively ugly.

Raising her hands, she pressed her palms against her cheeks in a gesture he could not understand. And then, as if some pull beyond control moved her, she walked forward, her clumsy

skirts catching and holding on the branches, into
the shadow of the trees. Once well hidden by their
overhanging branches, she paused once more,
standing very still, her head raised. She did not
appear to be looking, only waiting, listening. For
what Naill could not guess.

Timidly, shyly, her hand came up again to pluck
a spray of flowers. She cupped the blossoms in her
fingers, bending her head as if she studied some
treasure. With a glance over her shoulder, furtive
and guilty, she tucked the flowered stem into the
front of her robe. Her head up again, her eyes
sought now along the green-silver curtain of the
woods.

"Ashla?"

The girl's whole body jerked in answer to that
call. Her hand went swiftly to the flowers, pulled
them loose, and threw them away in what was a
single motion of repudiation. Then she was busy
adjusting her mask. When she turned to face the
child, that covering was safely in place. She
beckoned the little girl to her, looked into the
other's basket.

"You have done well, Samera," she approved,
with a warmth in her tone that had been lacking
when she answered the garthmaster. "Tell Illsa
and Arma that you may all eat a handful your-
selves."

The child's masked face was raised. "Is it
allowed?" she asked doubtfully.

"It is allowed, Samera. I shall answer for it."

When the child left, Ashla went back to her
picking, moving closer to the laden branch that

dipped above the trap. Naill's eyes smarted; the sun broke through here and there—dazzling, too dazzling for his altered sight. Yet he must witness what might happen now. Would she find it? Or would the cache be left for the discovery of a laborer who came to grub up the brush?

The bramble moved closer to her as she tugged it and stripped berries in double handfuls. Then her hands gave a harder tug, bringing up all of the long branch. She stood very still, masked face bent groundward. Her head turned; she glanced in the direction of the children. But they were half hidden, their dull dresses only patches between the bushes. She stooped and caught up a dead branch, dug into the earth with short, quick jabs.

Green fire flashed in so bright a spark that Naill winced, hand to eyes. When he was able to see again, she was holding the necklace before her. No expression could be read behind the enveloping mask, but she had made no sound, given no call to summon the men. Instead she spread out the necklace so its lace of gem drops hung smoothly in graduated rows. Naill, who had given that part of the treasure only passing attention before, could now observe and appreciate its full beauty. If the jewels were real, that garth girl now held a kingdom's ransom, such a necklace as an Empress would wear to her crowning. And he had no reason to believe that they were not stones of price.

Almost as if she had no control over her own desires, Ashla drew the lovely thing to her so those connected rivers of rich green fire now lay on the sacking stuff of her robe, making the coarse material twice as ugly in contrast. Maybe she thought that too, for she quickly held the stones away again. Then, to Naill's surprise, she balled the necklace and wrapped it in a big leaf culled from a nearby plant, tying it into a packet with a twist of grass.

One more glance at the children to make sure of their continued inattention and she pulled her skirts free from the clutch of the bushes to walk on into the woods. A sandaled foot came out from under her voluminous clothing as she dug with heel and toe into the leaf mold, dropped in her prize, and then pulled a stone over the hiding place. It was so speedily and deftly done that Naill might have been witnessing an action performed many times before.

Ashla gave a last searching inspection, then hurried back to the bramble. With her digging branch she recovered the rest of the treasure and was stripping the remainder of the berries when the children came straggling by with their own baskets.

"Ashla!" The call came from the garthmaster, and one of the children caught at the girl's skirt. She nodded a brisk reassurance in that direction and started out of the glade, the children in her wake, heading toward the open fields.

So—even the Believers were not immune to the temptations of the treasure traps! Naill remembered the story of the girl at Kosburg's who had kept running away to the forest until the Green Sick put an end to her "sinning" forever. Had she also secreted some part of a treasure, kept it hidden as he had tried to do, as this Ashla was attempting?

The ring of axes, the loud voices of the workers marked a change of direction. They would soon reach the bramble patch—too near his own lurking place. He must slip farther back into the wood.

Naill found shelter where the ring of axes was only a very distant sound and slept out the rest of the day, rousing after dusk to find a stream and drink. He still had a supply of bread from Iftsiga's supplies and he ate that slowly, savoring its flavor. There was no moon tonight; the wind was soft, moisture laden. Rain coming soon....

It might be wise to hole up again and wait out any storm. Yet he wanted to know—had the cache been discovered by those in the clearing? Would they have a guard there now? Or could their fear of the forest by night be determent enough?

Naill approached the clearing with stalker's caution, testing the air with his nose, listening to every sound, as well as using his eyes. The stone Ashla had left to mark the necklace was undisturbed. But beyond, the brambles had been grubbed away and...

He caught the enemy scent. Luckily the wind blew in his direction and not away. Ready for trouble, he dodged back in the forest and an instant later heard the coughing bay of a hound, followed by excited shouts from at least two men!

A guard right enough, reinforced by one of the watchdogs. But Naill did not believe they would dare to track him far; their superstitious fear of the thickly treed lands would be doubled at night, and he was certain they had not actually sighted him. The settlers at Kosburg's, at least, had been active in populating the inner woods with unseen enemies. The hound's uproar might be attributed to the prowling of an animal. No hunt would draw them this far.

But guards at the clearing meant that the cache had been discovered, that tomorrow or the next day or the next—whenever the garthmaster could summon a Speaker—the sinful objects would be ceremoniously destroyed and the "sin" of the whole small community purged by fasting and ritual. It would be best to lie low until that was over.

Yet—he had to know if his guess concerning the treasure trap was correct. Would Ashla follow the pattern—fall victim to the Green Sick, be exiled as a contamination, finally become what he was? He must know!

Why? Who? The questions still rode him. But more important—what was he to do now? Return to Iftcan to wait? Or...

In that moment Naill learned that one should never forget the forest was not all friend.

He plunged forward in a sprawl in the same instant that his nose was assaulted by a most stupefying charnel reek. Rolling, kicking, unable to free his right foot from a loop of dark ropy stuff, he hung at last head down and feet up against the wall of a pit, the stench from which turned him sick.

Kalcrok! Ayyar memory identified the enemy, the method of its attack. Naill twisted, trying to bring up his head and shoulders, the sword now free in his hand. He gained purchase with his elbow against the wall, enough to wrench his shoulders partly around. But he had only a second to bring out the sword point before the phosphorescent bulk on the other side of the hole moved.

The thing came in a flying leap meant to plaster it against the earth of the wall with the dangling body of its prey flattened under it. The very force of that spring brought its belly down upon the sword Naill held.

He cried out as claws scissored at his legs, as the terrible odor of that body, the disgusting weight of its mass struck against him. Then, as he hung gasping and choking, there came a thin screech, so high in the scale of sound as to cause a sharp pain in his head, and the kalcrok fell away, kicking and scrambling in the noisome depths of its trap, taking his sword, still in the deep belly wound, with it.

Naill, very close to unconsciousness, dangled head down once more. Then Ayyar memory prodded him to weak effort. To hang so was to die, even if the kalcrok had also suffered a death blow. He must try to move.

There was a bleeding rake across one arm; his legs were torn, too. But he must get free—he must! He twisted and turned, rubbing his body against the wall.

Perhaps the force of the kalcrok's spring had already weakened the web cord that held him, or perhaps his own feeble efforts fretted it thin against the rough wall. But it gave and he slid down into the debris at the pit bottom.

The gleaming lump that was the terror of that trap lay on its back, its clawed legs still jerking, the sword hilt projecting from its underparts. Naill retched, somehow got to his feet, and stumbled over to drag his defiled blade free. He ran it into the soil of the pit to clean it and looked about him half dazed.

To climb those walls was, he believed, close to impossible. They had been most skillfully fashioned to prevent the escape of the trapped. But kalcroks had back doors—they did not depend altogether on their pit traps to supply their food needs.

Only—such an exit would lead past the kalcrok's nest, and past any nestlings such a shelter might contain. Ayyar memory was clear enough to make Naill shudder. Move now—at once—before there was any stir there... if there were any to stir! He edged around the confines of the hole, supporting himself with a hand against the wall. The pain of his leg wounds was beginning to bite now. He must go, before those wounds could stiffen and keep him from moving at all.

This was it—a hole into blackness, from which issued a fetid odor to make him sick again. Forcing down his fear and repulsion, Naill went to his hands and knees, his sword ready, and crawled into that passage.

The walls were slick with slime, well polished by the kalcrok's constant use. This was an old, well-established den; all the more reason to fear a nest! And here the dark was such that his night sight, good as it was, could not help him. Scent? How could one separate any one evil odor from the general stench of this devil run? Hearing? He must depend now upon his ears for any warning.

And to do that he must go slowly.

So he crept onward, sweeping the sword back and forth ahead, to assure himself that there was no opening on either side of the run, pausing to listen. A scrape of leg against earth, the moving of a body—would he be able to recognize that for what it was, the warning of a nearby and occupied nest?

Sword point met nothingness to his left. Naill stiffened, listening. Nothing—nothing at all. Were the infant monsters alert and waiting to make their pounce? Or were there any nestlings now? Naill dared not linger too long.

It was the hardest test he had ever placed upon his courage and will, that slow forward creep. His only defense against attack, the sword, he kept point out, aimed at the opening he could not see, behind which lay death, not sudden, but very terrible.

The sword point bit at wall again—he had reached the other side of that opening. Now—now he must go forward with his back to that, never knowing when attack might come. This was an endless nightmare such as he had once awakened from in the past, shaking, wet with terror sweat.

On—on—no sounds...no, no sounds from behind. An empty nest—but he still could not be sure of that or count on such fortune. Relief could make one careless. Be ready, listen—creep—

though how he could turn to fight in this narrow passage Naill did not know.

Then, abruptly, the surface under him angled sharply upward and he drew a breath deeper than a gasp. This was the exit! Up—up and out! He dug the sword into the earth, used it to lever himself out... to be met with rain full in his face, cold and slashing on his body. And not too far away he heard the torrent of the river. The river—and beyond: Iftcan!

Did Ayyar take over wholly then? Naill afterward thought so. It was as it had been when the fever held him—small broken snatches of dream action wrapping him round. Or were they real, those times when he clung to river-washed rocks while a swollen stream rose about him, when he staggered on through gusts of beating rain with lightning flashes showing him the towering dead of the tree city?

There was one crash of thunder, blast of lightning bolt so great, so dazzling, that together they blacked out the world. And from then on he had no memories at all.

Trees—Iftsiga! He lay looking up into the might of the ancient citadel, its silver-green crown so far above him that the leaves were only a haze of color against the sky—as high as the stars almost.

The Larsh! Naill sat up, reaching for his sword, looking about him for some sign of the enemy. His body hurt—battle wounds. He had survived, then, the overrun at the Second Ring.

"Jagnal Midar!" His call issued from his lips a weak whisper.

A swish of displaced air overhead. He held his sword ready. Wide white wings, which clapped to body as talons touched earth—a quarrin came to him, a pouch dangling from its beak. "Hoorurr!" Naill loosened his grip on the weapon hilt. Once more he blinked awake from a dream Ayyar had known. "Hoorurr!"

The bird dropped the pouch by his hand, snapped and chittered a reply. Then the quarrin walked slowly down the length of the man's body as if inspecting his clotted wounds. Naill *was* back—in the safety of Iftcan—though he did not remember anything since he had crawled out of the kalcrok's den.

The storm that had raged in the forest as Naill won free from the kalcrok pit did not quickly blow itself out. His wounds tended with the same salve that he had used on Hoorurr's seared wing, he managed the climb into Iftsiga and lay there on the mats as the living wood of the chamber walls about him throbbed and sang with the fury of the gale.

Once there was a crash, heavier than the roll of thunder, and the whole of Iftsiga quivered in sympathy until Naill feared that an earthquake shock had threatened the rooting of the citadel. He guessed that one of the long-dead tree towers had been struck by lightning and wind-toppled.

There was no way to mark the passing of time, no period of sun alternating with the welcome cool of night. Hoorurr shifted from chamber to chamber, closing his wings to clamber down or up through the ladder hole, visiting Naill, or withdrawing restlessly again. The quarrin was unhappy, resenting the imprisonment forced upon him by the storm.

Then Naill awoke to silence, aware as he tentatively stretched his legs that the healing wounds no longer smarted, that he could move with a measure of comfort. And the pound of the wind was stilled, the tree silent, no longer pressed or battered.

He replaced his torn and soiled clothing with fresh from the stores; swung up and out on the entrance branch to look out over the forest in the fading, pale, watery sunlight. The storm had indeed wrought changes. Those trees that had shown bone-gray among the shorter green of new growth had been shattered. Smoke curled from charred and smoldering trunks. To the west where that wasteland of evil stretched, there was a drifting murk, as if fire burned thereabouts.

From this perch Naill could see across the river through the storm-torn gaps of foliage. There was a new chill in the air. He had landed on Janus— how many weeks ago? Now as he tried to count that tale of planet-spent days, first in his head, and then childishly on his fingers, he found too many discrepancies. But he had been brought to Kosburg's in late mid-summer. The days were now

chilling into the fall season. And he knew from
what he had heard at the garth that when winter
gripped this land, it could be sere and bitter.

Yet—Ayyar memories again—there had been
other winters long ago when men had not been
bound to shelter against storm blasts and leaves
lingered, if more heavily silvered, until new
opening buds pushed them free in the spring. But
that had been before the death of Iftcan.

Now the garths must be preparing for the cold
season. And this past gale had brought with it the
first whispers of the autumn change. Naill was
glad for the cloak about him when the wind
reached exploring fingers to the branch on which
he sat. Winter—the leaves gone, the forest naked...then if there was a hunt, any fugitive would
have far less of a chance. Had it been approaching
winter that had sent the strangers from Iftcan to
the sea?

He bit on that, savored what it might mean, as
he might bite doubtfully on a newly discovered
fruit—to find it sour. Onc could remain here in
Iftsiga. But winter was the season in which the
garths burned off the Fringe. Fire so set was never
controlled as far as its spreading in the forest was
concerned. The farther the flames ate into the
woodlands, the better the settlers like it. And the
dead trees about here would make one great torch
of the whole dead city.

Somewhere to the west, nearer the sea...Naill
considered that move thoughtfully. And in so
going west, he could swing by the frontier garth—
see what had happened there to Ashla. Tonight—

no, perhaps a day's more rest...then with his wounds less sore, he could move fast and quietly.

That night he hunted with Hoorurr, the bird dropping noiselessly to buffet a borfund with beating wings and slashing talons until Naill's sword brought an end to the bewildered animal's life. The man kindled a small fire among stones, toasted lean flavorsome meat over the flames on sharpened sticks, and found the taste good after his long diet of bread from the strangers' stores, the berries and seed pods of the forest. This had been done many times, Ayyar memory told him— this was the old free life of the Iftinkind.

The third night after the end of the storm, Naill sorted carefully through the supplies in the tree chamber and made up a journey pack, which must serve him if he did not or could not return over a period that might run into weeks. Another change of clothing, including skin boots, the bread stuff, a pouch of healing ointment, a knife he found. During that search for supplies, he opened and investigated every box and chest in the upper chamber—but he did not touch those of the treasure room below.

There was a reluctance in him now to have anything to do with those objects. Almost he could believe the settlers' conviction that danger clung to the caches, and he had no desire to test that theory further. As he stood at the foot of Iftsiga before setting out, Naill was struck by a sudden feeling of peril, so intense only determined effort of will set him moving.

As he went, Hoorurr winged down the forest

aisle over his head, uttering a querulous, complaining cry. From quarrin to man a distorted message sped...danger! Naill paused, alert, looking up to the bird now perched over head.

"Where?" His lips shaped the same word his mind formed.

But the concept that answered him was too fragmentary, too alien, to provide any real answer. Only that the danger was not immediate, only that it was old, old maybe as Iftcan itself.

"Fire? Settlers?" Naill pushed his demand for knowledge.

Neither. No, this was something else. Then he got an answer that was sharper, clearer. From the west came the threat—out of the splotch of the wastes. Keep away, well out of that. Old ills dwelt there, which might spread again were they to awake. Awake? How? What? But Hoorurr provided no understandable reply.

"All right!" Naill agreed. "I go this way." He tried to mind-picture a southwestern route, back along the river, to the garth where he had seen Ashla.

Hoorurr's orb eyes regarded him measuringly. Now there was no flicker of thought from the bird. He might be considering Naill's reply, turning it over in his mind to compare with a conclusion of his own.

"Do you go, too?" Naill asked. To have the keen-eyed, winged hunter with him would mean doubled security. He had no doubt the quarrin's senses were far keener than his own.

Hoorurr's feather-tufted head turned on round

shoulders. The quarrin faced west—that west against which he had just warned. Now his wings mantled as if he were about to launch at some prey—or some enemy—and he hissed, not cried aloud. That hiss was filled with cold venom and rage. He was a figure of pure defiance.

For it was defiance! Hoorurr was posturing against something to be feared. Again Naill tried desperately to reach the quarrin's mind, to learn, to share in what information was locked in that feather-topped skull.

With his wings folded neatly against body again, talons scraped along the branch as Hoorurr sidled to a point directly above Naill's head. The quarrin gave voice once more, this time with no hiss, but a clacking of beak the man had come to learn was a signal of assent.

They found the river high, the rocks necklaced with foam. Debris loosened by the storm rafted down with the current. To Hoorurr the crossing was no problem. He flapped over to a tree on the opposite bank. Nail moved along the shore, studying the lie of the rocks and calculating the possibility of using them as stepping stones.

Once there had been a bridge there, its arches long since tumbled and riven apart by numerous floods. Perhaps only Ayyar memory could have moved Naill's eyes now to pick up those points, align them, and see what way to take. A chancy path with the rocks wet, the water awash over at least two.

Settling his pack to balance evenly, he took a running leap. Somehow he made it—though he

was shaking with more than the chill of water
spray when he reached the far bank and sank to
his knees, a little weak and a great deal amazed at
the success of his efforts. On this side of the river
the storm rack was as evident. And, not having
Hoorurr's advantage, Naill had to make wide
detours to avoid the tangles where trees—not as
huge as those of Iftcan, but still large enough to
amaze offworlders—had gone down, taking their
lesser brethren with them. There was a wide path
of such wreckage cutting across the shortest route
to the garth, and the hour was past dawn before
Naill worked his way through that to take shelter
for the day.

When did he become conscious of that thin,
wailing plaint? The sun was no longer watery. Its
rays beat into the opening left by the storm winds'
fury, prisoning him in a half cave beneath
upturned roots. And the sounds of the daytime
dwellers of the woods were all about him. Small
creatures had come into the new open space to root
about in the disturbed soil.

But this sound . . . Naill lay with his head on his
pack listening, giving it the same attention that he
had afforded Hoorurr's warning. No, this was no
animal cry—no bird call! Low, continuous, wearing on the ears—and coming from some distance.

How long before he was able to associate that in
his mind with pain? Some creature trapped in the
snarl of wind-tossed wood, pinned between trunk
and earth, or mangled and left to suffer? Naill sat
up, hunched together, his head turning southward
as hearing traced that sound. Sometimes it sank

until it was scarcely audible; again its keening wail rose, broke, until he was sure he could almost distinguish words! A lost settler?

Naill crawled to the outer opening of his burrow, tried to shade his eyes well enough to see through the shattering brightness of the sun. He could just make out a mass of green several hundred yards away that the destructive path of the whirlwind had spared rather than flattened.

From there...or from beyond? Out in the open he would be as good as blind. But if he could work his way on to that other strip of standing wood, he might be able to make some progress. And the call—if call it was—pulled him, would not let him settle back into his hole.

Naill pursed his lips, imitated Hoorurr's hoot as he had learned to do in summons. The answering beak snap came from where the quarrin roosted in the upturned root mass over Naill's head.

"See—what—calls." The man thought that out, aimed the order at the bird. "See what calls."

Hoorurr snapped angrily, protesting. But he gave a hop to the next tree trunk and walked along it. His gray-white feathers made a blinding dazzle in the sun as he took off with a flap of wings. The quarrin preferred the night, but he could move better than Naill by day.

Naill tried to mark the shortest distance across that open space to the trees beyond. And always came that crying.

He shouldered his pack and moved out, squinting as he tried to avoid pitfalls underfoot. With one twist of his ankle that wrenched a half-healed

wound the kalcrok had dealt and that left him
limping, he made it across the open.

That crying—it did hold words, slurred together, undistinguishable, but words. And it came from
a point that could not be too far from the garth
fields. What had happened? Had the holding been
swept by one of the devastating winds, its people
driven into the forest they dreaded?

"One...alone...not right...."

Hoorurr's message came from up ahead. One
alone—but what "not right" meant was a puzzle.
Hurt—trapped? Neill plunged on. He came to the
edge of a glade—and understood.

That broken and forsaken hut Kosburg had
shown the newcomers as a warning, its moldering
ruins shunned by everyone on the garth—here was
another such, hardly more than a lean-to of brush.
Hoorurr perched on the highest point of its flimsy
roof.

Naill made a second rush across the open and
stooped to enter the place. The voice had fallen to a
muttering. He smelled the fetid odor of sickness,
and his foot struck against an earthen water jar,
which rolled away empty.

She had no mask, no hood now, and her sack
robe was torn so that her restlessly moving hands
and her arms were bare. The pallid skin was
splotched with great blotches of green, and masses
of loose hair had fallen away from her ever-turning
head. Her eyes were open, fixed on the brush of the
roof covering, but they did not see that—or
anything about her, Naill judged.

He slipped his arm under her, raising her rolling

head, steadying it against his own shoulder while he moistened her cracked lips from the water bottle he had filled at the river.

She licked her lips and made a faint sucking sound, so he let her drink more. Under his touch her skin was fire-hot, and she was plainly deep in the fever of the Green Sick. He settled her down once more and looked about the hut. The girl lay on a pile of torn and earth-stained bags, which must have been used for the storing of grain earlier. A plate was by the door, with some crusts on it and a mash of bruised fruit over which insects now crawled. Naill sent that spinning out with a grim ejaculation. Food—water—a bed of sorts! But what more could a sinner hope for?

In spite of the changes of the sickness, he knew her for Ashla. And Ashla must be a proven sinner by the rules of her own people.

Naill's expression was a half snarl as he glanced momentarily in the direction of the garth from which she must have been expelled as soon as they recognized the illness that had struck her down. But he had survived and, he suspected, so had others—perhaps many of them. There was no reason to believe it would be different for Ashla.

"Water—" Her hands groped out as if searching for the container she had long since emptied.

Naill helped her drink for the second time, and then wiped her face and hands with moistened grass. She sighed.

"Green—green fire..."

At first he thought she spoke of her illness, remembering his own delirium. Then Naill saw her hands were spanning apart, and he recalled how she had stood that day holding the beauty of the alien necklace before her in just the same fashion.

"Cool green of Iftcan..."

He caught those words eagerly. Iftcan! Did Ashla, deep in the clutch of the fever, now also house a changeling memory, know what had never been a part of the garth or of her own settler history?

On impulse Naill took her two hot hands into his, holding them tightly against her small attempts to pull free.

"Iftcan," he repeated softly. "In the forest—cool forest.... Iftcan stands—in the forest."

The restless turning of Ashla's head slowed. Her eyes were closed, and suddenly from beneath those lids tears gathered, made silken tracks down her sunken, splotched cheeks.

"Iftcan is dead!" Her voice was firmer, held an authority that surprised him.

"It is not—not all of it," he assured her softly. "Iftsiga stands, living still. Cool—green—the forest lives. Think of the forest, Ashla!"

Frown lines appeared over her closed eyes. The heavy brows that had given her face harshness were gone now, as was most of her hair. Naill wondered how close she was to the complete change. Her ears—yes, they were definitely pointed, larger than natural for the human kind.

Now her hands tightened on his, rather than trying to pull free.

"The forest—but I am not Ashla." Again that

note of firmness, of decision. "I am Illylle—Illylle!"
Some of that confidence trailed away.

"Illylle," Naill repeated. "And I am Ayyar—of
the Iftin."

But if she could still hear his voice, his words
meant nothing to her now. More of the tears ran
down her cheeks from beneath her lowered eyelids.
And her lips shaped a small, soft moaning, not
unlike the crying that had drawn him there.

Water—he needed more water. But to return to
the river ... the journey was too long to be made in
daylight. Naill shaped a thought for Hoorurr,
hoping the bird might guide him to some forest
spring.

"In the leaves—above," came an answer Naill
did not understand until he freed himself from
Ashla's hold and crawled into the glade about the
hut. The quarrin fluttered from the roof, reached a
tree branch well overhead, and moved along it
toward a cluster of differently shaped leaves the
man had not noticed before—some form of
parasite growing there.

The center portion of those drifting stem-
branches was a large rounded growth, not unlike a
bowl fastened levelly on the branch of the
supporting tree. Naill climbed, worked his way out,
and did indeed find a source of water—two full
cups or more held in that tough fiber basin—and
he filled his water bottle from its bounty.

He was in the hut again sponging Ashla's face,
when a sharp gasp brought him half around to see
a figure in the doorway. Masked and hooded, but

small—small as one of the girl children who had
accompanied Ashla to pick berries days earlier.
The newcomer held a basket before her, and now
she backed away—raising that as if to use it as a
frail barrier against some expected attack.

"No—no—please!" It was a shrill, frightened
wail, rising fast to a scream that held no words at
all. "Go—go away!"

She flung the basket at him, a water bottle
spinning from it to strike against his arm. Then
she stooped and caught up a clod of earth, letting
fly without aim.

"Let Ashla be—let her be!" Once more she
screamed.

Behind Naill, Ashla herself stirred. A hand
caught at his shoulder, as, without apparently
seeing him, she dragged herself up on the bed of
sacking.

"Samera—" Her voice was a hoarse croak, but
in it was recognition, a sane awareness.

The child froze, the eyes frantic where they were
framed by the mask holes. Then she screamed
again, this time touching a terror that was beyond
words.

She fell, twisted about, and scrambled away on
all fours, still screaming, the terror in those cries so
great that Naill was kept from any move after her.

"Samera! Samera!" Ashla swayed forward,
tried to crawl after the little girl. Naill caught her
shoulders, drew her back against him in spite of
her weak struggles. Now he partially understood
Samera's horror. The change in Ashla was almost
complete; he steadied a woman who was now as

much a changeling as himself. Ashla had truly
become Illylle of the Iftin and a monster in the
sight of those of her own kind.

TEN   ILLYLLE

Ashla's eyes closed; her head lolled forward as
Naill lowered her on the bed place. Samera's cries
still sounded, fainter now. That clamor—would it
draw others from the garth? He sat back on his
heels. The girl was changed enough to arouse fear
and aversion, as was seen in the child's actions.
The Believers did not kill—that was their creed.
But he had been hunted away from Kosburg's
garth by hounds that knew no law. And Samera
could touch off such a hunt here and now.

He could leave, could easily be away before the
hunt was up. But Ashla—to the settlers he owned

nothing. However, she was no longer a garth woman; she was one of his own kind. Could he rouse her enough to get her away?

"Illylle!" Once more Naill caught her hands, moved by some hope as he called to the Iftin part of her. "Illylle—the Larsh come! We must home to Iftcan!"

Slowly and emphatically he repeated those words, close to her ear. Her eyes half opened; from under the droop of those swollen lids she looked up, appeared to see him. There was no fear nor repulsion in her gaze, only recognition of a sort, as if he were what she had expected.

"Iftcan?" Her lips shaped the word rather than repeated it aloud.

"Iftcan!" Naill promised. "Come!"

To his surprise and relief, when he tried to raise her, she was more than able to get to her feet. If Illylle possessed Ashla's half-alien body now, she had the power they needed. But Naill kept his arm about her shoulders, steering her out of the hut, catching up his pack as he went.

She cried out and covered her eyes with her hands when they came into the open.

"Aiiii—there is pain!" Her voice had a different intonation.

"Do not look," he cautioned, "but come!" Naill half led, half supported her across the glade of the hut and into the forest beyond. At the same time he aimed a thought at Hoorurr.

"Watch—see if those come after!" He heard the whirr of wings as the quarrin took off.

Whatever spirit or determination supported

Ashla, it continued to hold, kept her tottering on. In fact her steps grew firmer as she seemed to recover balance and energy. How long did they have? Would Samera's outburst bring hunters behind them? Naill clung to the memory that Kosburg's people had told stories of "monsters" but never of capturing one—they were never followed far into the fastness of the forest they were reputed to haunt.

If he could get Ashla to the river, and beyond that barrier, he did not believe that anyone would follow them into Iftcan. The woodland they were now traversing was speedily pierced, even at their wavering pace, and now they had before them the opening the wind had slashed. To guide and pull the tranced girl through that under the sun... Naill doubted he could do it.

Though he listened, he had not yet heard any hound yap. And Samera's cries had been ended for long precious moments. Perhaps the child had been visiting the glade hut in secret, against the orders of the garthmaster. If so, perhaps her terror would not override the other and longer-held fear of household punishment.

"Close your eyes, Illylle," Naill ordered. "Here the sun is bright."

He had slung the pack thongs over his left shoulder; his right arm was about her fever-hot body in support. Now he squinted his own eyes into narrowed slits as he tried to steer them a course in and out among the tumble of storm-scythed growth. Here and there some broken canopy of withering leaves provided temporary sanctuary where they could halt and drink. And Naill could ease his eyes by swabbing a dampened cloth across the closed lids. He feared to pause too long, to allow his companion to slip to the ground, lest he could not urge her up and on again. But she walked more strongly, caught up in another world from which she seemed to draw energy. Her muttered words told him that she was now matching those dreams that had haunted his own fevered flight to Iftcan—now she was Illylle.

The sacking robe, hanging in tatters about her thighs and knees, continued to catch on broken branch stubs or in tangles of vine. She jerked out of Naill's hold, when he tried to pull her free from the third such noosing, and unfastened the belt and the lacings at the throat, dropping it to lie in a dingy circle about her scratched and dusty feet.

"Bad!" She kicked at the roll of cloth. "Ahh...." She stretched her arms up and out. A short, thin undergarment clung to her body.

Their struggles through the rough brush had rid her of the last straggling locks of hair, and under the sun the green pigmentation of her skin was complete. Before, judged by off-world standards, she had had no beauty, nothing but youth. Now, once you accepted the skin tint, the bare skull, the tall, pointed ears—why, she was fair!

Naill blinked from more than the excess of light. How deeply was Illylle now rooted in Ashla? Would she be horrified, frightened, when she learned what had happened to her—as he had been when he had first seen Ayyar's reflection in the pool?

A hound gave tongue and was answered by a leash fellow. Naill caught at her hand.

"Come!"

Her eyes flickered at him without any true awareness. She tried to pull free from his hold, shaking her head.

"The Larsh!" Naill traded on those alien memories. And it worked. She ran, heading straight for the next patch of woods, while he limped after past the tree roots where he had sheltered earlier. His twisted ankle hurt, and the half-healed wound in his calf throbbed as if a band of fire had been linked there. But the cool of the wood now cloaked them.

Perhaps Naill was a little lightheaded, too, or the Ayyar-memory grew stronger, for he felt that behind them snuffed and ran... not the hounds from the garth... but things that were not yet men, only held the rough outward seeming of men. He felt that he must reach Iftcan before the Larsh gathered for the final test of strength against strength, life against life.

There was a flurry of wings overhead. Hoorurr had come, and the thought that reached from quarrin to Iftin was a drawing cord. Naill stumbled into the green world as if he plunged from a fire-haunted desert into the body of the sea.

"Throbyn... Throbyn...!"

Naill's head turned as the cry acted like a sharp slap across his sweating face to arouse him. Ashla was backed against a tree trunk, her nostrils expanded as she drew deep breaths. In these shadows her eyes had a luminescence. But once

more there were tears on her cheeks, and she
smeared the back of her hand across them with the
gesture of a small child who has whimpered out
her hurt to meet no comfort.

"Throbyn?"

"Illylle!" Naill took a step toward her.

"You are not Throbyn!" Her accusation was
sharp. Then, before he could reach her, she was
gone, flitting down the tree aisles.

Kalcrok pit, faintness born of her fever, a fall—
all the dangers she could meet there alone sent him
limping on. Would the same homing memory that
had led him to Iftcan guide her north? The
river...it was in flood! If she dared a crossing
there unheedingly...!

"Hoorurr!" He appealed to the quarrin and
watched, with only a very small lightening of his
concern, the white wings beat after the vanished
girl, leaving him to hobble after.

His pack caught in the undergrowth, was a
delaying irritant, but he dared not, or could not,
bring himself to abandon it and the supplies. So,
juggling it into a better position on his shoulders,
Naill struck a crooked lope, which did not favor his
injured leg as much as it needed. Whenever he
drew a deeper breath than a gasp, there was a stab
of pain beneath his lower ribs, and he thought
longingly of the river as a spent swimmer might
watch the nearest shore.

"Here!" Hoorurr's call—came from the west.

Trouble of some kind. Naill risked further hurt
to leap a fallen tree, and struck left. That kalcrok
trap—where did it lie? Even with its dreadful

maker dead, the pit itself was a threat to the unwary. Had Ashla fallen there?

But Naill found her lying in a small dell by a spring, where drooping branches cut off the direct rays of the sun. She was crouched together, her arms about her knees, her head down upon them, her body shaken by shudders.

"Illylle?" Naill halted, called softly, not wanting to send her into another headlong flight.

At the sound of his voice her body stiffened, the line of her bent shoulders went rigid. But she did not lift her head or move.

"Illylle?" He took a step and then a second into the dell, not quite sure whether he could keep on his feet.

Now her head did come up—slowly. He could see her face. Her eyes were closed so tight that her features seemed twisted. Her mouth worked as if she screamed, yet she made no sound save the rasp of breath whistling in and out of her distended nostrils.

The pool! Now he knew what had shocked her into this almost mindless state of fear. As he had met Ayyar, so had she in this place seen Illylle's countenance for her own. Going down on his knees, Naill cupped his hands together and caught up a scoop of water, cold on his heated flesh. This he threw straight into her convulsed face.

Her eyes opened. First they held in a rigid stare as if she saw nothing but what had frozen her into close-locked fear—then that broke as she looked at him. And the increase of terror in her eyes, in her face, was frightening to watch. She squirmed

away from Naill, her mouth still writhing out
soundless screams. There could be no reasoning
with her at this moment; she was beyond the wall
shock had erected, deep in a place where sane
speech could not reach her.

Naill threw himself forward, locked his hands
around her thin wrists. She thrashed about under
his weight, but he pinned her fast. The quickest
and best way to deal with her might be to knock her
out completely—but he doubted if he could. She
was almost as tall as he, and her body had been
hardened and strengthened by labor. Thin as she
was, he could not carry her the rest of the way to
the river.

Somehow he got a lashing of vine about her
wrists and leaned away, panting, to consider the
next move. How far was the river? Naill tried to
place landmarks about him. And then he heard the
hounds again—faint, to be sure, but with an
exultant note in their cry. They had picked up the
fugitives' trail, knew the scent was fresh. He hoped
they were still leashed.

There was no heading directly for Iftcan. Even
if Ashla came out of her present state of shock, and
was eager and willing to make that journey with
him, he doubted if they could recross the stream
there. And if she must remain a desperate prisoner,
it was worse than useless to try.

Westward there was a portion of the river he had
passed on his way to the sea. Where the bed
widened, the waters, even when storm-fed, would
run more shallow. But—that fronted the waste
that Hoorurr had warned against.

They could cross there, keep close to the riverbank, and so avoid all but the fringe of that waste—or turn completely west to the sea and abandon the seeking of Iftcan. That, Naill decided, was the wisest course.

Ashla huddled down, her bound hands pressed tightly against her, her eyes wide and wild as she watched his every move. But she no longer tried to scream. If he could only bring Illylle's memory to the surface of her mind again!

"Illylle!" Naill did not try to touch her, made no move toward the shaking girl. "You are Illylle of the Iftin," he said slowly.

Her head shook from side to side, denying that.

"You are Illylle—I am Ayyar," he continued doggedly. "They hunt us—we must go—to the forest—to Iftcan."

Now her mouth worked spasmodically. But he did not believe it was a scream that could not win free. She made a small choking sound, and her tongue swept across her lips. Then she lunged, past him, to the side of the pool, hanging over the water and staring down at her reflection there. From mirror to man she glanced up, down, up. Apparently she was satisfying herself that there was a resemblance between what she saw in the water and Naill.

"I—am—not—" She choked again, her wailing appeal breaking through her hostility.

"You are Illylle," he responded. "You have been ill, with the fever, and you have had ill dreams."

"This is a dream!" she caught him up.

Naill shook his head. "This is real. That"—he

waved a hand southward—"is the dream. Now—
listen!"

The baying reached their ears.

"Hounds!" She identified that sound correctly,
glanced apprehensively over her shoulder. "But
why?"

"Because we are of the Iftin, of the forest. We
must go!"

Naill shouldered the pack, caught up the end of
vine dangling from the binding on her wrists.
Briefly he wondered why it was so important that
he take her with him, away from her kin. Only they
weren't her kin any longer, that hunting party
coursing "monsters" with their hounds. They were
changelings together, he and she, their loneliness
so halved. He had known loneliness in the Dipple
when Malani had fallen ill and strayed so often
into her chosen dream escape. But the loneliness
he had known when Ayyar claimed him had been
the worst of all.

"Come!" That was an order. When he saw that
she could not easily rise, he drew her up to him. She
shrank in his hold, her face a little averted as if to
escape looking directly at him. What if she never
accepted the change?

Naill started on, pulling at the vine tie. She
came with him, her eyes half closed, her mouth set.
But she held to his pace; she did not drag back.

"You are hurt—there is blood..."

Naill was startled at her first words. He had
stains above the boot top on his bad leg, but they
were already stiff and drying.

"I was caught in a kalcrok pit." He answered

with the truth, wondering if Illylle's memory could supply the rest.

"That is an evil creature, living partly underground," he added. "The wound was healing. I fell and opened it again."

"This kalcrok—you killed it?" Her question was simple, such as a child might ask. "With the big knife?" Her bound hands gestured toward the sword in the sheath of his sword belt.

"With the sword," Naill corrected absently. "Yes, I killed it—because I was lucky."

"You have lived here always—in the forest?"

"No." Naill took the chance to drive home the idea of the fate they shared. "I was a laborer—on a garth—and I found a treasure."

"A treasure," she interrupted, still in that childish tone. "Green and pretty—so very pretty!" She had her hands up, trying to pull them apart as if holding the necklace once more. "I had one too—green—like the woods."

"Yes," Naill conceded, "a treasure such as you found. Then—then I had the Green Sick—and afterward I was Ayyar, though I am also Naill Renfro." Could he make her understand, he wondered.

"I am Ashla Himmer. But you called me by another name."

"You are Illylle—or in part you are Illylle."

"Illylle." She repeated the name softly. "That is pretty. But I sinned! I sinned or I would not now be a monster!"

Naill took a chance. He stopped short and turned to face her.

"Look at me, Illylle!" he commanded. "Look well—think. Do you see a monster? Do you truly see a *monster*?"

At first it appeared that she might answer that with a ready affirmative. But as his gaze continued to hold hers, steady and with all the demand he could put into it, she hesitated. Frankly she inspected him from bare-skulled head to mudstained boots and back again.

"No—" she said slowly. "You are different—but you are not a monster, only different."

"And you are different, Illylle, but you are not a monster. You are not ugly. For an Iftin you are fair—not ugly, just different."

"Not a monster—not ugly—for an Iftin, fair." She repeated that wonderingly. "Please"—she held out her bound hands—"loose me. I shall not run, you who are Ayyar and also a sinner named Naill Renfro."

He slit the vines and threw them away. Her acceptance had come more quickly and more completely than he had dared hope a short time before.

"Tell me—do we go now to a city, a city of trees? I think I remember those tree towers. But how can I?" she asked, disturbed.

"Iftcan. Yes, there is such a city, but much of it is now dead," Naill told her. "What you remember is from long ago."

"But how—and why?" She asked his own questions of him.

"How—I can guess in part. Why"—Naill shrugged—"that I do not know. But what I have

discovered is this." As they went he told her of
what he had found in Iftsiga, of the treasure buried
at her own holding, and of all he had learned or
suspected.

"So—those who sin by taking the forbidden
things"—she summed it up in her own way—"they
are punished—by becoming as we. And so the
Forest Devil does tempt us, even as the Speaker
has always said."

"But is that so?" Naill countered. "Is this truly
punishment, Illylle? Do you hate the forest and are
you unhappy here as you would be if this was a
punishment?" He was arguing awkwardly, perhaps, but he was sure he must alter her rationaliza-
tion of the Believers' creed and her application of it
to their own problem. If she believed that the forest
was a punishment for the damned, then for her it
might be just that.

"The Speaker said—" she began, and then
paused, plainly facing some thought, perhaps not
new to her but one of which she was still wary. She
stopped short and put out her hand to the tree
beside which she stood. It was an odd gesture she
made, as if her warm flesh curved about a loved
and beautiful possession. "This—this is not evil!"
she cried aloud. "And the city of trees, of which I
dreamed, that is not evil! But good—very good! To
Ashla there was evil—to Illylle good! For Illylle
there is no Speaker, no one to say this is bad when
it is good! So"—she was smiling now, looking at
Naill with a light in her eyes, on her face, the light
of one making a discovery of a new and joyful
freedom—"so now I am Illylle for whom the world

is good and not filled with sin—always so many, many sins, so many sins where the Rule holds the listing."

Naill laughed involuntarily, and a moment later she echoed him. It was as if some of that feeling of joy had winged between them. At that moment Naill felt no weariness, no pain. He wanted to run—to cry aloud in this new feeling of freedom and delight.

But behind, the hounds bayed, and striking deeply into his mind came a warning from Hoorurr.

"They come faster, forest brother—go!"

Naill caught at Illylle's hand and started on at the best pace he could muster.

ELEVEN   TO THE MIRROR

The sun that had plagued them was veiled by dull
clouds. Illylle was looking out over the open
riverbed. By her shoulder Hoorurr perched on a tall
rock, his head turning from Naill to the north and
back again slowly, while he snapped his bill in
small sharp clicks of dissent.

Across the water lay a rock-paved shore where a
mist—or was it smoke from smothered fires?—
curled in languid trails.

"What lies there?" she asked.

"I don't know. But—"

"It is evil!" That was no question, rather a

statement of fact. The girl raised both hands to her
head, bent forward a little, her eyes closed. Naill
laid fingers on her upper arm.

"Are you ill again?"

She shook her head. The quarrin stirred,
regarded the girl with a surprise as open as that
which might be expressed on human features.
From Hoorurr's throat came a series of small
purring notes, which Naill had never heard before.
The quarrin's feet lifted, first right and then left, as
if he were engaged in some solemn dance in time to
his own calls.

And now Naill saw Illylle's head move too,
slightly but unmistakably in that same rhythm,
back and forth, in time to Hoorurr's stamping feet
and muted cries—or was the quarrin taking his
lead from her? This was something Naill could not
understand except that within him the conviction
grew that at this moment the leadership of their
small party was passing from him to her.

"No!" He tried to catch at her arm once more.
But she was already gone, flitting ahead, to splash
into the river shallows, wading out in the main
current. Hoorurr voiced a great hooting cry and
spiraled up, circling above the river and the girl.
There was nothing for Naill to do but follow.

Illylle pushed on without hesitation, as if she
knew just where she was going and why, swerving
to avoid storm rack, yet always coming back to a
line that would bring her out on a rock ledge on the
opposite shore. One of the mist trails drifted over
the water, and Naill caught the reek of smoke: true
enough, smoke from a fire fed by vegetation. Thin

as that was, it made him cough and was raw in his nose and throat.

The girl scrambled up on the ledge, going on all fours to reach the crown of the slope. Hoorurr continued to wheel overhead, but the quarrin called no longer. At the top where that rock shelf leveled, Illylle halted and stood straight, her wet garment clinging to her body above her scratched and welted legs. She faced north, inland, her arms hanging to her sides, her eyes now wide open—yet, Naill believed, not fixed on any visible point ahead. She was either seeing farther than his own sight reached, or something that was within her own mind.

> "Gather dark, gather dark,
>   Bring the blade, bring the torch—
>   Summon power the land to walk."

Her voice was very soft, close to a whisper, and she accented the words oddly, chanted them into a song without music.

"Hooooorurrrr—" the hooting cry of the quarrin was her answer.

As Naill pulled himself up to join her, she turned her head, and once more he saw the luminous spark deep in her now wide-open eyes.

"The power is thin, perhaps no longer can it be summoned." Her words meant nothing. Maybe she had plunged so deeply into Illylle memory he could no longer reach her.

"Come." He faced east—toward Iftcan.

"That way is closed." Now it was her hand that

held him back. "The barrier thickens." There was
for a moment a slow smile on her lips. "No warrior
steel cuts a path through the White Forest."

"What—?" Completely bewildered, but realizing that her cryptic warning was indeed seriously
meant, that Ayyar memory stirred in him at the
mention of the White Forest, Naill hesitated.
"How, then, do we go?" he asked.

Illylle's head lifted; her nostrils quivered.
Through the dark mass of the cloud bank broke a
flash of lightning. And the wind sang along the
river with a wild, rising voice.

"They gather—oh, they gather! And the power
is thin—so thin!"

Naill lost patience. To be caught in the open if
the coming storm proved as severe as the last one
was folly, perhaps close to suicidal. They would
have to find cover. He raised his voice to top the
wind: "We must have cover from the storm!"

She caught his hand and began to run west,
along the rock ledge bordering the river. He found
that he dragged back as his wrenched leg stiffened, slowing the pace she set. Then she studied
him, came to some decision of her own.

"...not...run..." Her words were tattered by
the rising wind. They were both lashed with whips
of water from the river. Her pull was insistent as
she angled abruptly from the stream edge straight
into the murky portion of the wasteland. Naill
strove to hold back, to argue.

His earlier distaste for that country was
hardening into something a great deal stronger
and more militant.

"To the Mirror—the Mirror of Thanth!"

Ayyar memory ... for an instant he had a mind picture of silver, rimmed with pointed rocks. A place of power—not Forest Power, but power! Then that was gone, and the wisp of meaning it held for him vanished as the wind about them swept the mist murk out of their way, cleaving a clear path into the dreary overgrowth of the waste.

Naill was moving faster before he noted that what lay underfoot now was not the broken earth with its trap-tangle of vine and vegetation, but a pavement of gray stone, very old, with dusty hollows and grooves worn into its surface as if for many centuries feet had trod here. Old—and alien to even Iftin kind—but not forbidden.

Illylle ran a little ahead, having dropped his hand when he followed. There was an eagerness about her, not only in her eyes, in the curve of her lips, but in every line of her thin body. She could be one hastening to a long-waited rendezvous ... or home.

The pavement was not wide, and in places sand and earth had silted over it so that only the faintest traces were discernible. But the girl never looked down at where her feet trod; she watched ahead—seeking some other guide, or perhaps already moved by one.

Dark—the dark was drawing in. And with it ... Naill's eyes moved from side to side. His night sight could not reach far enough in the storm's gloom. There were shades—things—which could be bushes swaying in the wind ... or something else. Only none of those deceptive bushes touched

upon the roadway, nor did they approach it too
closely. It was framed by rock and bare earth.

And those rocks, mere rounded boulders at first,
looked entirely natural in this grim country—until
they crowded more thickly at the road edges, rising
in rude walls, first waist high to the fugitives, then
even with their shoulders, and on to tower above
their heads, until those giant slabs on either side
let in only a slit of sullen gray sky far above. Naill
believed now they were a wall built with purpose—
to protect the road, shelter those who used it?

Down in this trough between those rock ridges
the wind was gone, but now and then a distant
play of lightning could be seen. Rain began,
funneled down upon them by the rock walls,
running in streams to join a widening rivulet
about their feet, ankles, calves.

"Illylle, if this water rises..." Naill broke out.

"It will not. Soon we come to the Guard Way."

"Where do we go?" He tried for enlightenment
the second time.

"Up"—she sketched the direction with a rising
hand—" to the Mirror. To the Earth's Center."

She was right; the road was rising, becoming
steeper. But still it ran north and they must be well
into the waste. No murk clung in this cut, nor did
Naill smell any of the reek the drifting mist had
carried. Here was only rock washed by the rain.

Now Illylle slackened pace. "The Guard Way—
have you the word?"

"No." Naill stared ahead eagerly. The rocks in
the wall arched, met to form a dark mouth of what
might be a tunnel. There was shelter from the

storm, but there might be other things to consider past temporary comfort of body. For some reason Naill's hand fell to his sword hilt; he drew the blade.

Slim silver in the gloom. A speck of green danced on its point, brightened, flared as if he bore a torch. Then Naill saw on the rock of the arch other green flecks come to life, flash but not die. On the sweep of the keystone a symbol waxed into life—glowed.

Illylle laughed. "Not dead—not dead—sleeping only—to awake—awake!" Her voice arose in a cry of triumph.

> "Starlight, swordlight, Ift-borne,
> Welcomes back the wanderers.
> Far travel, sleep long,
> But the Power returns...."

She swung about, standing now under the vast curve of the arch with its glittering green symbol, held out her hands to Naill in a wide gesture of welcome.

"Sword-bearer, give me your name!"

"Naill Renfro," one part of him said with a desperate stubbornness. But he answered aloud, "I am Ayyar, tree borne in Ky-Kye—Captain of the First Ring of Iftcan."

"Sword-bearer, come, be free of the Guard Way."

They were faced by a stairway in place of the road, a stair that climbed up and up under the rock roof, leading where Naill could not guess. And the Ayyar memories did not supply an answer here.

Together, shoulder to shoulder, they climbed those stairs. And as Naill faltered and limped, Illylle lent him her strength. There was a feeling of serenity and comfort that flowed from her arm under his, her nearness, into his tired body, keeping him climbing.

How long was that stairway? What space of time passed as they climbed it? They were outside normal time in a queer way Naill Renfro could not have produced words to explain, but which Ayyar found right and natural. Around him was the past, and any moment now some barrier would break, and the past would flow in upon both of them. Then they would know all the answers, and there would be no more questions to ask.

Only that did not happen; the end of the stairway came before they broke that intangible barrier. They came out into the open once more on a straight, smooth ledge in a cup, which might have been the cratered cone of a small volcano. Stark walls rose from a sheet of untroubled water, a silver mirror that did not reflect the light—for there was no light overhead now, not even a prick of star—but rather contained a glow within itself, as if it were a pool of fluid metal.

"The Mirror!" Illylle spoke softly, for they were in truth intruders, disturbing something vast— beyond human comprehension—something so old, so full of power, that Naill flung up his sword arm, hand still weighted by the drawn blade, to hide his face. Her fingers were warm on his wrist, drawing it down once more.

"Look!" she commanded, and in that order was such authority that he must obey.

Mirror still, mirror bright—vast as an ocean, small enough to be scooped up by his two hands—it spread, it shrank, it pulled, it repelled. And under all Naill's emotional stress—fear and awe—there grew an aching hunger. What he desired most did not come. Again there was a barrier between him and what waited just beyond, something so wonderful, so changing of spirit, that he could have cried aloud his loss and frustration, beaten down that wall with his sword. All knowledge was there—and he could not reach it!

Through his own depths of desire and sorrow Naill heard Ashla crying. And that sound drew him back to sight and awareness, not of what could have been, but of what was. The girl crouched on the ledge above the Mirror as she had beside the forest pool where the consciousness of her changing had first come to her. But there was no terror or horror here. No, like him, she was torn by the loss of what she could not have, for all her reaching.

Naill knelt beside her and drew her into his arms. Together they took comfort from the fact that this overwhelming failure was shared, was a part of each of them.

"What have we done?" she whimpered at last.

"It is what we are," he replied, and knew that he spoke the truth. "We are only a part of what we should be to stand here. We are Illylle and Ayyar, but we are also Naill and Ashla. So we are neither truly one or the other—to fear wholly . . . or to have all."

"I cannot—" She drew her hand across her tear-wet face and began again. "How can one go on—

knowing that this is here and yet one cannot have it? We have been judged and found wanting."

"Are you sure that will always be so—the judgment is final?" Naill had begun that as reassurance; now he wondered for himself, too. "Suppose—suppose"—he put his groping into words and the words were like water to a sun-dried traveler, bringing their own comfort—"that Illylle and Ayyar will grow the greater, Naill and Ashla the less. It has been a very little time since we were changed."

"Do you believe that in truth, or is it only words said in kindness?" she challenged him.

"I meant them as words to be kind." He felt compelled to the strict truth in this place. "But now—now I believe them!"

"This is the Mirror of Thanth. And in it is the Power and the Seeing. Someday—perhaps the Seeing will be ours then.... And, oh, the richness of that Seeing!"

"Now"—Naill arose and drew her up with him—"it is better that we go."

Ashla nodded. "If I could only remember more—the way of the Asking and the Giving—"

"I do not remember as much as you do," Naill told her quickly.

"But you are a warrior, a Sword-bearer—for you it is the Giving, not the Asking," she burst out impatiently and then stood, hands to lips, as if startled by her own words. "Only bits do I remember...but once—once I knew it all! Illylle will come back fully, *then* I shall know again. But you are right. For us now this is a forbidden place. We have escaped the Wrath only because we came with clean hearts and in ignorance!"

They went down the stair, but when they reached the gate of the Guard Way, Naill slipped and lowered himself stiffly to the stone pavement under its arch.

"I do not think I can go any further, whether I provoke the Wrath or not," he told her simply.

"And I do not believe that shelter here will be denied us," she returned. "Give me your sword— for again I remember, a little."

She took the weapon by its leaf-shaped blade and laid it flat on the pavement directly beneath the archway. "The key will keep open the way."

Then Ashla opened Naill's pack, exclaiming over its contents. Together they ate of the bread, drank from the bottle he had refilled at the river. Naill's last waking sight was of Ashla shaking out the extra clothing, measuring it against her. He drifted to sleep, his head pillowed on an Iftin cloak. Outside, the murmur of running water on a road older than man-kept time was a soothing lullaby.

A glowing sword before him—a warning. ...Naill moved, his shoulder grating painfully against a rock wall. He sat up. There was a sword on the floor, yes, and it was glowing—not green, as it had been beneath the gate, but coldly silver. He laughed. That was the reflection of daylight—pale, yet bright enough to be caught by the highly polished blade.

A stir on the opposite side of this nook and Ashla also sat up, to blink drowsily back at him. She was dressed now in the extra suit of hunter's wear, and she had belted on the long knife that had been at his side before he went to sleep.

"You are well?" he asked, hardly knowing what greeting to use.

"There were many dreams," she replied obliquely. "I have a feeling we will do better away from this place."

Now that she had put it into words, Naill was sure of the same thing. There was a chill in this stairway, the belief that intruders were not welcome—that they should be long gone. He strode back and forth to test his leg. Some of the stiffness held, but he could move—if limpingly. Naill broke a piece of bread in half and shared it with her.

"Back to the river now," he began. Yes, back to the river, then west to the sea. They must find those others who had set the traps. Then they would know—as they must—the purpose behind all this.

"Back to Himmer's garth."

At first Naill was so intent on planning his westward journey that those words did not register in his mind. When they did, he stared at her. "In the Forest's name—why?"

"Samera," Ashla replied as if that made everything clear.

"Samera—the little girl?" Understanding was still beyond him.

"Samera—she is my sister. When they took me to the forest to die—as they thought, a sinner judged—she came with food and water. They would beat her for it if they discovered. Perhaps she is now sick, too. I must know, do you not see that? I cannot leave Samera! The new wife—she is the keeper of the House Rule now. Me she hated, and to Samera she was unkind always, for we are children of the first wife. While I was there I could stand between her and Samera. But now—now Samera is alone, and she is too young to be alone!"

"To Samera you are now a monster. It was she who put those hunters on our trail." Naill spoke the truth brutally, because it was the truth.

"That may be so. But still—I cannot leave Samera!" And he knew she was set in her stubbornness. "There is no need for you to go back with me," she continued. "I can hide in the forest, try to reach her by night."

"She would not come with you. She would be afraid."

"She would know me, and knowing me, she would not fear."

"And how would you get into the garth yard at night, find a child kept indoors? The hounds—watchers—they will be alert now for anyone coming from the forest."

"I know only that I cannot leave Samera—she will be lost without me."

"Listen—I am telling you the truth, Illylle. We are no longer of the same breed as your sister. You will not know her as you did; she will not know you." Naill spoke out of the wisdom he had gathered upon his return to Kosburg's. This girl would feel the same revulsion.

"In this I am still Ashla, not Illylle. I go for Samera!"

Naill set his teeth as he remade and shouldered a smaller pack. "Then, let us go."

"For you there is no need," she told him quickly.

"There is a need—we go together or not at all."

TWELVE

FIRE HUNT

"Tell me—why do you do this?" Slim in the forest dress, Ashla was almost one with the twilight shadows as she halted briefly between two drooping-branched trees. So much had she bent to Naill's will that they had gone west for a space instead of directly south, that they might approach the Himmer garth from that direction, thus taking what precautions they could against any sentries along the Fringe.

"Why do you seek Samera?" Naill countered.

"She is my sister. For her I am responsible."

"You are Ift, I am Ift—in that much we are now kin."

"Not blood kin," she protested. "You can go on to the sea, find those others who you spoke of. This is no work of yours."

"Can I?" Naill asked deliberately. "Am I sure there *are* others of the Iftin after all? What proof have I? Some tracks, too loosely set to be sure of more than that something walked erect through sand and on earth; a signal on a cliff already burned to ash when I reached it; sight of a log floating out to sea.... No, I have seen no Iftin—I have only guessed and pieced together a story, and what I guessed may be very wrong."

He heard her breath catch, saw her head turn toward him.

"But there have been others with the Green Sick—others left such as we."

"How many?" he pressed.

Ashla shook her head. "I do not know. The illness was a punishment sent to sinners. No garth wished to publish the guilt of its people aloud. We would hear whispers of this one and that struck down. But of my own knowledge I do not know of more than five."

"Five—from this district alone?"

"From the south Fringe line—and that was in five years."

"A steady drain—but why?" He repated the old question. "I wonder.... How many in all the years since a first off-world landing was made here? And are all those now ... Iftin?"

"You are free to search and see," Ashla pointed out swiftly.

"I am not free. I stay with the Ift I have found.

But in return I ask one promise."

Her chin lifted. "With Samera there, I promise nothing!"

"Then just listen. If you find that what you wish is impossible—that you cannot reach her, or that she will not come—then will you go without lingering?"

"You are so very sure she will not come with me. Why?"

"I cannot make you understand with words— you will see for yourself."

"She will come—if I can reach her!" Ashla's confidence was unshaken. "The dusk is now full. May we not go now?"

Hoorurr had vanished when they had taken the road to the Mirror two days earlier. Naill wished for the quarrin now. With the bird scouting before them, an invasion of the garth would not have seemed quite so foolhardy. But lacking Hoorurr, they must depend upon their own eyes, ears, noses.

He had earlier forced one concession from Ashla: that she would follow his orders in the woods until they reached the fields. And the girl kept that promise faithfully, obeying his commands and copying as well as she could his woodscraft. There was no moon showing tonight, and the softness of coming rain was again in the air.

"The cold may close in early this year," Ashla observed as they crouched together in a thicket. "When there are many severe rainstorms earlier, that is so."

"How early can it come?"

"Perhaps within twenty days, a sleetstorm, after that others, each worse...."

Naill shelved that future worry for the action at hand. "Listen!" His hand on her shoulder was a signal for quiet. The yap of a hound ... they heard it clearly.

"From the garth," she whispered.

Naill's tension did not ease. One dog might be at the homestead; that did not mean that others were not patrolling the fields, accompanying a human guard. He said as much.

"No. To those the forest at night is a place of terrors. And Himmer is a cautious man; he will have all in the holding, the gates barred."

"But you plan to enter there." Naill thrust home the folly of her proposed move.

For the first time since she had made her decision at the foot of the Mirror stairway, Ashla's resolution showed a small crack. "But ... I must." What began hesitantly ended in the firmness of a vow.

"Where in the house would Samera be?" Naill recalled his own expedition at Kosburg's when he had looked upon beings with whom he no longer had any common ground.

"All the little girls—they sleep together in the loft. It has two windows." Ashla sat back on her heels, plainly attempting to visualize what she described. "Ah—" She turned to him eagerly. "First there is the covered shed where there are two phas colts. And from the roof of that, it would be easy to reach the window. Then I can call Samera—"

"And if she sees you?"

After a moment of silence her answer came, a small ragged note disturbing her former confidence. "You mean—she will fear me—cry out as she did at the hut? But perhaps it was you she feared then. Me—I am Ashla who loves her! She would not fear me! And also, it is dark in the loft; they have no light there. She will hear my voice, and of that she will not be afraid."

Perhaps there was some logic in that argument. And—short of dragging Ashla away bodily, which he could not do—there was nothing left but to yield to her desire and do the best he could to take all precautions possible.

They circled farther to the south in order to move into the wind. There was only one wan light showing at the garth now—the night lantern in the yard. As far as they could judge, the inhabitants of the household were safe abed. The field crossings were made in rushes that took them from the shadow safety of one wall to the next. Then they were close to the stake barrier about the buildings.

Naill's nose wrinkled against the smell of the garth and its people. Just as the human scent of Kosburg's larger holding had awakened revolt in him, so did the odor of this place. And this time the impact of his olfactory senses was even sharper. He heard a small gasp from his companion, saw her run her hand vigorously under her nose.

"That"—Naill tried to drive the truth home—"is the smell of off-worlders!"

"But we—we are—" She was shaken, bewildered.

"We are of the Iftin, who do not kill trees or live encased in dead things! Now do you begin to believe that we are we—and they are they?"

"Samera can be like us also!" she said obstinately. But Naill thought that she eyed the bulk of the buildings before her a new way—certainly not as one returning to a familiar place.

The phas shed was set against the stake wall, or they would never have made the entry. A running leap took Naill within grasping distance of the top. Once up, he lowered his sword belt to aid Ashla's climb. Below them they could hear the stir of the animals, a snorting from one of the beasts. Ashla lay flat on the roof and crooned softly, a soothing rise and fall of small notes. The snorting stopped.

"They will be quiet," she whispered. "I fed them their mash, they know my voice. And—there is the loft window!"

Still on her hands and knees, she scuttled across the shed roof and crouched beneath the opening. Then she arose slowly to look inside. Her survey took so long that Naill wondered if the dark baffled her sight, better than human though it was. Then, even as she had quieted the phas colts, so she signaled again—a small hissing of whisper, the separate words of which did not even reach as far as his own post. Three times she spoke. Naill caught a glimpse of movement within. The windowpane swung out and a child stood there, her arms reaching for Ashla.

Only, when Ashla's hands went out in return, the child shrank back and Naill heard her frightened cry.

"No—no—not Ashla—a demon! A demon is here!" Her screams were as wild as they had been in the forest clearing. Naill moved, crossing the roof with a wild thing's leap to catch at Ashla, force her back with him to the wall drop.

"Over!" He threw her rather than let her climb, following in an instant. There were other sounds in the garth. Just as his expedition to Kosburg's had aroused that other holding, so were Samera's screams doing here—and now the hounds' bay drowned out her cries.

"Run!" Naill caught Ashla's hand, and they were well on their way across the first field before he was conscious that she was not dragging back, that her flight was as quick and sure as his. But she was sobbing as she fled.

"Not—not—" She fought to get out words Naill believed he already knew. "Not Ashla," she choked out. "Never Ashla again!"

His own revolt against Terrankind had been complete, but he had had no ties with anyone at Kosburg's beyond a kind of passive companionship. How much harder this must be for someone who had to learn that even close blood ties no longer held between settler-born and Iftin. Would the shock be as great this time as it had been when she had faced Illylle in the forest pool?

The main thing was to get away, back into the shelter of the woods. The garthmen might bring the hounds out in the fields, patrol for the rest of the night in the open, but that they would venture far into the forest he doubted. And he intended to be as far to the westward as possible before the coming of dawn.

"You spoke the truth," Ashla said as Naill swung her down a gully, pushed her along that cut. "That was Samera and we—we were no longer sisters. She—she feared me, and when I looked upon her, it was as if she were someone I had known long ago but for whom I no longer felt in my heart. Why?"

"Ask that of those who set the treasure traps," Naill retorted. "I do not know why they must have their changelings—but changelings we are now. We have no longer any contact with off-worlders."

"It was so with you?"

"Yes. I tried to go back to Kosburg's when I recovered from the fever, after I was changed. When I saw them I know there was no going back."

"No going back," she repeated forlornly. "But where do we go?"

"West—to the sea."

"Perhaps that is as good a place as any," she agreed mechanically. And she did not speak again as they plunged deeper into the wood.

They kept on past the dawn, since the day was cloudy. Though no rain fell, yet there was a mist in the air and this turned chill, so they were glad of the hooded cloaks. Wearing these, they melted so into the general green-silver-brown of the forest, Naill thought any trailer without hands would pass them directly without noticing.

The river had taken a bend to the north, and they had not yet reached its bank when Naill learned he had underestimated the enemy to an extent that might mean their deaths. A flyer's hum grew loud and with it the crackle of unleashed energy. Rising smoke and fumes marked the beat of a flamer whip wielded from on high! The pilot was cruising hardly above treetop level, using on the shorter forest growth of the river bottoms a portable flamer.

In spite of the dampness of the mist, the recent rains, no vegetation could resist that. And a fire so begun would burn until a storm of hurricane proportions would be required to quench it. No longer depending upon their own hunting methods, the garthmen must have appealed to the port officials for aid. If he and Ashla could be thus herded into the open by the river, they would be easy prey.

The ruthlessness of that flame lash was enough to panic a fugitive. Naill forced his fear under control.

"What is it?" The girl's attention was for the way they had come, the smoke, the sound of crashing trees as the ray ripped the wild.

"They have a flyer and are using a flamer from it." Naill reported the truth.

"Flyer...flamer..." She was bewildered. "But those are Worldly weapons—no garthman would use them."

"No—so they must have called the port officials."

"How could they? The Believers do not allow

com units in any garth—those also are Worldly."

"Then the port police were already out—for some reason."

There had been that other flyer hunting over the river when he had first made his way to Iftcan. But that was days ago. Why would they still be patrolling the wild? Hoorurr had been wing-shot by a hunting party in the forest. Had that party failed to return? Such a mishap could explain some of this.

Nor did it matter now how they had come; the fact that they were methodically lashing the forest with their destructive ray was the danger. And about the Iftin fugitives other creatures were taking flight. A small pack of borfunds burst through brush, running beside Naill and Ashla for several feet before they plunged again into a thicket. Birds fluttered from tree to tree, and other things swung or winged from branches, moving north before the fire.

"What—" Ashla halted, stripped off the cloak to roll it over one shoulder so it would not impede her flight. "The river—we head for the water?"

Naill longed to agree that that was their salvation. But he could not be sure—not with the flyer above. Oddly, he never thought of attempting communication with the pilot of that craft. The mutual repudiation between changeling and settler had been so complete that he had no hope of any understanding from the off-world officials of the port. The river it would have to be.

They made for that, pushing their weary bodies to the limit of physical endurance. Luckily, the

flyer pilot was engrossed in laying a crisscross
pattern of rays. Ashla stumbled, nearly went
down, her breath coming in huge, tearing gasps.

"Can—not—" she choked out.

"Can!" Naill cried with a confidence he did not
feel. His ankle was paining again. But ahead was
the river. As he pulled her to her feet, he held her so
and demanded: "Can you swim?"

She shook her head. A shaggy animal hardly
smaller than a phas lumbered past them, its heavy
shoulder fur actually brushing against Naill's
arm. The man began to run again, pulling the girl
with him, in the wake of the animal, which blasted
an open path straight through the underbrush.

Somehow they made a bank ten feet or so above
the waterline. The shaggy animal had gone over,
to half wade, half swim into the deeper part of the
stream where other life splashed. All were heading
downriver in a wild and vocal mixture of life forms
Naill found largely strange. The forest for miles
must have emptied its population into the dubious
safety of that strip of water.

"We can't go in there!" Ashla clung to Naill,
watching the struggle below with wide and
terrified eyes.

Naill glanced across the river. The murk that
hung over the waste was there stronger, thicker. In
it he could see gleams of red he was sure marked
flames. Even if they could win over there, passing
among the battling animals, they would not be
able to go ashore. In the water, a chance—over
there, no.

"We have to!" he shouted in her ear, propelling

her to the rim of the drop. "There—" he pointed to a piece of driftwood bobbing between two rocks, at any moment ready to be plucked out of its half mooring. "Get your arms over that. It will keep your head above water."

But they were to have no time for a careful descent of the bank, a chance to choose the method of their water entry. A garble from behind, the whiff of an only too familiar odor—Naill whirled half around, his outflung arms striking Ashla full in the back, to send her over the lip of the drop.

In the dark of the trap pit he had seen a kalcrok as it normally appeared to its victims. Here Naill faced a half-grown specimen of the same horrible species running in the open. The silky hair growth on its back shell was scorched away; it must have lingered in its den until the last possible moment, perhaps having had to break through a flame wall to escape. The pain of those burns must feed its natural ferocity into madness.

Naill used his cloak as a flail, beating at the head of the creature. The cloth was torn from his hold, and he stumbled back, over the cliff. He had one moment of knowing that he was falling.

Then he landed in a pocket of sandy gravel, his left arm under him, with enough force to drive the breath out of his lungs in an explosive puff, and he lay there dazed. From the ground above sounded a snarl spiraling up into a yowl. Sand and soil sifted over the edge, but the kalcrok did not leap after him.

Shaken and weak, Naill got to one knee. Ashla ... where was Ashla? A barrier of rocks rose between him and the small cove where that floating length of drift had lain. He thought his forearm must be broken. But he crawled sidewise along the stones to look for the girl.

There was a place of disturbed earth, marks leading to the lapping water. But those could have also been made by one of the animals. And the drift piece still bobbed by the water-washed rocks. No sign of her! Suppose she had hit her head, slid helplessly on into the steam?

Naill crept to the water's edge, but before he had a chance to look, a mass of reddish fur, torn and running with a brighter red from gaping wounds, rolled down from above. A fanged jowl dropped to emit one of those snarling yowls as the creature hit water, floundered, and then was washed on to sway limply against the very piece of drift which was to have supported Ashla.

There was just enough strength left in Naill to make him crawl on, away from that small cove. The dim hope that the girl might have gone so, instead of into the water, kept him going. Then came the sound of a motor hum. A remnant of self-preservation flattened him face down on the earth. Naill lay there, whimpering a little as the waves of pain flowed from his arm, pulsed through his body—until he hardly cared that any moment the flamer ray could hiss across him.

Inside him grew a full and sullen hatred for that off-worlder flyer—for all the species who killed trees, burned the land. These—these were of the Larsh breed! Should he live, by some miracle, should he come out of this fire hunt—then there would be a harrowing of these new Larsh, such a sword-feasting as the ancients had never seen! He was Ayyar and this was Iftin land—while still he lived, it was Iftin!

Pain.... The flamer ray? No, that would have finished him. And the flyer had passed over. For this small space—this very small space of time— an Ift had won, if the mere preserving of one's life was a victory.

THIRTEEN   THAT WHICH ABIDES—

THIRTEEN

"Ayyyyaaaarrrr—"

His cheek scraped gravel as his head moved. Why was he so aware of that small discomfort amidst the haze of pain that wrapped him in? The Kalkrok—he had fought a kalcrok—won free of its pit. No, that was wrong; he had faced another kalcrok on a riverbank and had fallen...

"Ayyyyaarrrr!"

Against his will his eyes opened. There were smoke wreaths over him, the choking fumes making him cough. That coughing wrenched his body, bringing gasps of pain. Heat came with the smoke; scorching fingers of it reaching him. Water...there was water....

Naill began to crawl until the one hand he could use plunged into that water. Then, without knowing just how, he rolled into the stream, floundering, his head under so that he choked again.

"Ayyar!"

Something pulled at him. Naill tried to fight away from that clutch, which was torture as it tightened on his arm.

"No!" He thought he shrieked that protest.

Water.... Naill was in the water, but his head was above it, resting on a support that moved, spun, pulled him with it first in one direction and then another. But the haze had cleared some from his head; he was able to look about him with a measure of comprehension.

His injured arm lay along a water-worn log; his right one dangled across it into the water on the other side so that his head and shoulders were above the surface of the river. And when with infinite labor he was able to turn his head, he saw he was not alone. Green-skinned face, the eyes very large, and bright, pointed ears above a hairless head.

"Ayyar?" She made of his name a question. But as yet Naill could not answer; he could only lie quiet, letting her will and the river's current decide his future. That somehow he had found Ashla, that they were in the river—that Naill knew. The rest did not matter now.

There were other creatures in that waterway. A dripping head arose beside Ashla's for a space; a clawed paw strove to cling equal with her hands.

Then both vanished again without Naill's really knowing what manner of animal had striven to share their very frail hold on the future.

"Ayyar—push!" Her voice roused him again.

Smoke—or dusk? The river was dim. Before them loomed a land tongue sprouting rocks and tangles of brush. On that were beached other fugitives from the water. Some still squatted above the waterline, others moved inland. The bottom rose abruptly under Naill, and his knees scraped on that undersurface, jarring his arm so that he cried out.

They crawled up among those other refugees from the fire. There were many rocks here arching high, and they squeezed into a pocket between two such. Naill collapsed; only the boulder backing his shoulders held him up.

"Your arm—" Ashla bent over him. "Let me see."

Red hot agony was a lance reaching up into his shoulder, down into his chest. He tried to evade that torture, but her body was braced against his, her two hands cupping his chin, holding his head steady as she spoke slowly, striving to gain and hold his attention, to reach his thinking mind.

"The bone is broken. I shall try to set it. Brace yourself so—and so...."

Her hands were on him, shifting him a little, his right hand put against a rock, palm flat. Dimly Naill understood, tried to do as she wanted. Then—pain to which what he had earlier felt was nothing at all! He swirled away wrapped in that pain, losing the rocks, the stable earth under him—everything!

There was a weight across his body, a throbbing in his arm. Naill raised his head. Light—growing light. . . . His eyes squinted and then he forced the lids further up. The weight on his chest was his left arm splinted and bound. And the light was that of day.

"Illylle!" She had been with him in the river; that held through the haze and pain. And now she slid down a boulder at his call. In one hand she carried a leaf-twist container from which water splashed. As she held that to his mouth, Naill drank thirstily.

"Can you walk?" Her hands were under his shoulders, trying to raise him. She spoke brusquely, her question a demand.

"There is need?" Naill was alert enough now to measure what might trigger her concern.

"There is need."

He was on his feet, a little lightheaded, but ready to move. Matter-of-factly Ashla came to him, drew his right arm across her shoulders, and started him along between the rocks.

They appeared to have come ashore in a barren waste. No green showed, and the rocks glittered in the growing light. They would have to find a refuge from the sun or be blinded until evening. But where?

"Where do we go?" Naill asked her, hoping for some concrete answer.

"Up." Her reply was ambiguous. But climb they did, and that was a chancy business, though they went slowly and the terrain was rough and broken enough to provide a kind of natural stair in places.

They finished that climb on a height facing broken lands riven by crevices out of which curled, as might tongues of green smoke, twisted spires of vegetation, more gray than green, Naill's eyes told him. And there was no promise here of a welcoming forest. Suddenly Naill stiffened against the girl's steadying arm.

"Which side of the river?" He asked that with more emphasis than he had used before.

"The north."

"This is the waste." He did not need any confirmation from Ashla. The very feel of the place caught at him as might a breath of corruption out of a long-sealed kalcrok pit. All he could see were rocks and those ravines choked with ill-shaped growth. Yet—as he had before on the road to the Mirror—he sensed a lurking, a scouting—a spying. Not on his part, or Ashla's—but something . . . out there. . . .

"This is a waste," she repeated almost stolidly. "But the sun is rising. We cannot return to the river. And twice the port flyer has cruised overhead."

There were strong arguments for going to ground here, yet still they were weak ones in the face of what Naill felt as he looked out over this barren country and remembered Hoorurr's warning. They had gone undetected, unharmed, to the Mirror, and returned. But all through the latter part of that journey, Naill had known with a strange certainty that safety lay only on the ancient road between those two walls, walls that had been erected with a purpose of defense...against what? And that road had been so very old—could the menace it had been walled to resist still exist?

"There is no choice," Ashla continued, and Naill could feel a tremor in her arm about his shoulders. "We need not go far—and you have your sword."

Naill saw now that the belt of that weapon weighed down her shoulder. Where she had found it, or how she had kept it through their river journey, he did not know. But he believed that in this time and place that Iftin-forged weapon was small protection indeed.

However, they had no choice. Perhaps he could make the shade of the nearest of those knife-slashed crevices go to ground under its growth to wait out the day. But that was the best he could do.

"Get me over there." He pointed to the nearest cut. "Then you go, keep close to the water and head as far west as you can before true sunrise. I do not know how far this extends—and you may be able to get out in an hour's travel."

She made no answer as she steered him ahead. What he suggested had only a small chance of success, but it was better, far better, than for her to remain here.

When Ashla did speak, it was to point out the easiest way down into the ravine, to warn against rough footing. And Naill was too engaged with battling through brush to argue with her. The stuff was brittle, oddly desiccated, as if, in spite of its appearance of life and growth, it was really dead and only preserved a semblance of what it had once been in truth.

There was an acrid smell to the snapped branches, crushed leaves, not the wholesome aroma of the forest country. As they neared the bottom of the cut, Naill saw pale, unwholesome plants close to ground level, puffy things with fleshy, tightly curled leaves.

"Here." Ashla steered him right and halted. Part of a tree trunk still possessing a look of the true forest protruded from the wall of the gully, its heart long since decayed and eaten away, but its outer shell making a kind of wooden cave, which, to Naill, offered more natural roofing than the still-living vegetation about it.

But when he put out his hand to that old bark surface, he touched not the substance of long-dead wood, but the hardness of rock. The tree was petrified.

"This will serve me," he told the girl quickly. "You must go, before the sun climbs."

She had eased him down under the curve of the stone bark. Now she settled herself beside him composedly.

"We go together—if at all."

Naill was alert to that hint of foreboding.

"If at all?"

All at once Ashla bent her head, covered her face with both hands. He was sure she was not weeping—not with running tears. But there was a kind of despair in the line of those hunched shoulders, that gesture with her hands, that held a hint of fear. Only for a moment did she sit so, and then her head came up, her hands dropped to lie on her knees. But her eyes remained closed.

"If—if it were only given me to remember—to know!" She cried out, not to him, Naill believed, but to the very circumstances of their being. "Illylle knew—so much she knew—but Ashla does not. And sometimes I cannot reach Illylle through Ashla! Naill, what do you know of Ayyar, truly know?" Her eyes opened, held his with a fierce intensity as if his answer was now the most important thing in the world, could lead to some salvation for both of them.

And it sparked in him a need to search his own mind for Ayyar and what Ayyar of the Iftin had known.

"I think"—he spoke slowly, wanting to be very sure of every limited fact, if fact could be the term for a recollection; he did know—"he was a warrior—and he was Lord of Ky-Kye. But the meaning of that I do not remember. He was a Captain of the First Ring at Iftcan, and he battled there when the Larsh overran the Towers. He was a hunter and one who roved much in the forest. That is all I am sure of. Sometimes I pick a fruit, cross a trail, see or hear some animal or bird—and know what Ayyar knew of them. But of Ayyar I know very little."

"Enough knowledge to keep you alive in the forest, and a little, very little, more than that," she summed up.

Naill straightened. That—that made sense in a new way!

"Perhaps that was all Ayyar was meant to give

me!" he burst out. "Enough forest lore to keep me alive! And all the rest—all that about the fall of Iftcan was something that was meant to be forgotten but was not!"

"If one has a recorder and must leave a message in a hurry"—Ashla caught up the tossed ball of his idea—"and the message lies in the middle of another report, then one could push an emphasis charger, but still part of the report would intrude upon it."

"A recorder?" Naill was surprised that she would choose such an example to illuminate her meaning. "But were recorders used by the Believers?"

"No. But when my mother had a blood affliction and the Speaker could not pray it away, her father—Bors Keinkind—came and took her to the port to see the off-world medico. I went with her, for she was unable to care for herself. But it was too late—had we gone earlier she might have been saved." Ashla was quiet for a moment and then went on. "It was there I saw recorders and many other things...things to make one think—and wonder. Many times have I remembered and thought on what I saw there. But suppose this forest lore was important for survival—so you were given part of an Ayyar memory...and other parts of that memory also clung."

"What about Illylle? Does she also furnish you with such aid?"

"Yes—knowledge of animals, foes to dread...of certain plants to eat, to use in healing"—Ashla

frowned—" and some that may be weapons. But—
Illylle was once a person of power. She knew of the
Mirror, and she had a right to stand above it and
evoke—evoke what lies within its waters. I think
she was in some manner a Speaker of her people,
one with weapons and tools not to be seen or felt.
And it is in this place that I sense that the most,
because I want to hold those weapons."

"Against what?" Naill demanded.

Her frown grew. "I do not know!" Her hands
went again to her head. "It is locked in here, I know
it is! And it is very important that I remember what
Illylle knew. There is danger here—worse danger
than the flamer, or the hounds and the garth
hunters. It has rested a long time—or slept—or
waited with patience... and now—" Dropping her
hands, she faced Naill with a dawning horror far
back in her eyes, and her voice sank to the faintest
thread as she finished that warning. "It would—
feed."

Naill found himself listening, not with just his
ears, but with all of him—as the hunted listen for
the snuffling of a hound. Yet he knew that no
animal, no man, threatened them. It was something older, far more powerful, far more complex
than any life form he had known before. Was it
already out there, teasing them? Or had it not yet
awakened, become aware that what it so long had
hungered for was now within reach?

"The White Forest!" Illylle spoke now, and
Ayyar's fear flared at that name. "This is the
Fringe of the White Forest!"

"Iftin sword, Iftin hand,
Iftin heart, Iftin kind.
Forged in dark, cooled by moon,
Borne by warrior who will stand
When Ring breaks and tree tower falls—
Iftin sword—Iftin brand!"

trailed into silence from the rich swing of that chant, a chant that carried in its cadence the march of feet, the clash of swords, the purr of tree drums.

"Iftin sword!" she echoed, and with a swift movement drew the blade he had found at Iftsiga. " 'Forged in dark, cooled by moon!' If it were so—if it were only so!"

"That was part of Ayyar memory," Naill told her. "Do you know its meaning?"

"A little—only a little. It is a prophecy, a promise—made to an Iftin hero in the Blue Leaf day. And it was fulfilled. But that was in the Blue Leaf, and our leaf is Gray and withered." She turned the blade over and over in her hands, studying it closely. "This was a key at the Guard Way—we saw that, both of us. Perhaps it is more than a key. Perhaps it is the blade of Kymon, or akin to that blade. If so, it has a power in its own substance. Illylle, Illylle—let me know more!" The last was a cry that was close to a sob.

Naill took the sword from her. True—he had watched that green spark flare on the tip of the blade and the symbol glow in reply on the keystone of the arch. But in his hand he could see no more than a finely made weapon.

"What did Kymon do? Was he the hero of the prophecy?"

"Yes...it was so long ago—dim in memory. He dared the White Forest and won the Peace of the Iftcan, so that those of his blood could tower the Great Trees. And that which nourished the White Forest was bound by the Oath of Forgetting and Side-sitting. Then the Blue Leaf became the Green, and still the Oath held between Iftin and That Which Abode Apart. But when the Green Leaf was at its falling, the Iftin were fewer and That Which Abode stirred. The Oath was called aloud before Iftcan, so that the waste dared not advance. Only the Larsh—who had not sworn the Oath, because in the day of its uttering they could not mouth words—answered That Which Abode and came into Its light. And so they were established as a nation and grew the greater as the Iftin grew less.

"When the Gray Leaf budded, once more That Which Abode stirred and the Towers of Iftcan were shaken. The Oath was spoken and the Burning Light could not pass. But the Larsh, who had not given the Oath, became Its hands, Its weapons, and the Larsh were many, the Iftin so few, so very few...." Her hands were up before her, slightly cupped, fingers apart. Almost, Naill could see her try to hold water that trickled away to be swallowed up by thirsty earth. And in him Ayyar responded with a vast surge of anger and despair.

"Then came the end of Iftcan and the end of the Iftin. There was no more Oath-binding and That Which Abode was freed to do as It willed with Its servants—the Larsh."

"And this is the memory of Illylle?" Naill asked softly.

"This is the remembering of Illylle, though it comes to me dimly as one sees through hot bars of sunlight. Now—the Larsh.... Is this the Day of the Larsh, the Night of the Iftin having passed?"

"I think that perhaps the Day of the Larsh has also passed away. There is no tale of them since the first off-world ship put down on Janus a hundred planet years ago."

"The Larsh may be gone, but that which sent them has not! Old powers linger in this land!" Her voice grew stronger. "This may not be the blade that was forged by Kymon, carried by him into the great Sword-feasting of the White Forest. But within me is the knowledge that it has its power, and"—she paused, then nodded, as if she had been reassured by some voice or thought Naill could not share—"that you have a part in what is to come, a part of purpose. Now—it is well into day, and day is the time of That Which Abode. We must have rest. Give me the sword, Ayyar-Naill, and do you sleep, for in me there is a stir, and perhaps I can remember more—whereas if I sleep, I may lose—"

Her certainty was such that he could not protest. As Naill settled himself on the ground, the disconnected story she had told held in his mind— Kymon, a hero who had forced the Oath upon the Enemy, so that the trees of Iftcan could harbor his people, and the ages that that Oath had held back a burning, pitiless white light, until the Iftin grew too few—too few and too thin of blood-line, too burdened with ancient memory to maintain their fortress and their lives against the battering waves of Larsh, new-come from the beast and daring in their youthful ignorance, their fostered hate, to destroy that which they could never build, stamp out what they did not understand. Yes, Ayyar memory told him, she had the truth of that... Illylle-Ashla, Mirror Watcher that was.

FOURTEEN

CAPTURED

The bared blade lay across his knee, his good hand resting ready on its hilt. Naill sat quietly. Outside the vegetation-filled cut, the land was baking hot under a blazing sun. But here, within the trunk of the petrified tree, he could see. And always there was hearing to depend upon for warning. Ashla slept now, curled on her side, droplets of sweat gathering on her forehead. For if the eye-blinding glare of the sunlight did not reach here, the heat it generated did.

He had nothing to do but listen and stare out at the stretch of gully. Where the sun reached in splotches, the thick, fleshy growths opened,

flattened out their leaves, ate. Naill watched
insects, small creeping things, blunder onto those
leaves, stick fast, be slowly absorbed into the
unwholesome surfaces. This was a place alien to
man in its very nature.

The country of the forest had been closed to the
settlers, feared and hated by them, but home to the
Iftin. This was a land closed to all life, save that
which had been conquered—or had bargained and
accepted the Enemy's terms. To Naill's eyes it was
dead or dying. But that was not the truth. No, the
life of the waste was merely frighteningly different.

Ayyar had given him hunter's ears, a forester's
sixth sense. Now Naill was conscious of a stir, a
kind of awareness. Then he caught a clicking,
regular—faint at first, then louder, then fainter
again. As if something had passed along the upper
rim of the gully, something that had no reason to
slink, or creep—something patrolling on sentry go.

Perhaps he was allowing his imagination too
free rein. Yet Naill's senses were as certain of that
as if he actually watched the thing pass there. The
fugitives were to be kept in the pocket until—? That
"until" might mean many things—an attack in
force, a break on their part, the coming of higher
authority.

Ayyar memory supplied Naill with no picture to
match that clicking pace. It was louder again,
coming now from the other lip of the ravine. Either
the sentry was making a circuit of the gully—or
there were two of them.

The wise thing might be to break cover while

there was only one sentry—or pair of sentries. But
neither of the fugitives dared try that. They would
be blinded by the sun, unable to either fight or run.
Some flying thing was planing down to skim just
above the growth in the gully.

Hoorurr? Naill, for an instant of time, held a
very forlorn scrap of hope and so was tricked into a
half betrayal. He tried thought-contact with that
flyer. And in return met a force so outside his
comprehension that it was a monstrous blow,
hurling him back against the curve of the tree-
trunk wall. Not a flying thing, he thought
groggily, but an intelligence, and entity using a
smaller and weaker thing to discover—him!

"No!" Perhaps Naill screamed that; he could not
tell—perhaps he only resisted that invasion, with
mind alone. But he was no longer in the tree. He
was out in a space he could not have described in
any words he knew—confronting a being, or an
intelligence, that had no form, only force and alien
purpose, a being to which he and his kind were an
enigma to be discarded because they did not fit the
pattern the being created.

And it was the very fact of that alienness that
was Naill's shield of defense now. For he sensed
that there was something in him that baffled the
enemy, struck into the very heart of that overwhelming confidence.

"Ky-Kye!" The old battle cry was on Naill's lips.
"Naill!"

His head was against the petrified wood.
Ashla's hands rested on his shoulders. Her eyes
held to his as if by the power of that intent gaze

alone she had pulled him back from the place where he had faced the Enemy.

"It stirs! It knows!" Her features were set, stern. For a long moment her gaze continued to hold his as if she thus searched into his mind, seeking some thought, some feeling that should not be within him. Then her head moved in a small nod.

"The old truth stands! *That* may kill, but it cannot break us—even when one is Naill-Ayyar instead of true Ayyar."

And he answered strangely, out of thought that was not yet clear. "Perhaps because of Naill-Ayyar, not in spite of Naill."

She caught his confused meaning. "If so—that is well. Made to lose old knowledge, we should gain some measure of return. But now ... *that* knows of us!"

Naill edged along the trunk's interior. He did not know whether he could sight either of those sentries—that which clicked, or that which flew. Ashla lifted a hand in warning, pointing up.

The winged scout or spy was still above and now it gave voice. Not with the carrying hoot or beak-snapping of the quarrin, but in a long, shuddering wail, more suitable for stormy skies and high winds than for the sunlight of open day. And—across a piece of open sky—Naill saw it fly. Saw—what? He was not sure. The light was too strong for his eyes. And that thing could almost be a drift of cloud. He only knew it was glittering white and its form hard to distinguish.

"Not a bird ... I think." He qualified his first guess.

"It is a Watcher and a Seeker...." Ashla brushed the back of her hand across her forehead. "Always only bits of what should be known. In itself it is not to be feared—only that it is an extension of That Other...."

"Listen!" Naill shaped the word with his lips, afraid that even a threat of whisper could reach the sentry. The clicking—from the opposite side of the gully.... He eyed the brush about the mouth of the tree trunk, measured the distances and the height of the growths, before he began to tug at the lashing that fastened his injured arm across his chest.

Ashla would have protested, but he signed what he would try and she loosened the tough ties of grass, leaving his arm free. Naill began to squirm a few inches at a time into the open, out of the protecting hollow of the tree.

No clicking now—the sentry had passed, was at the farther end of the gully. But Naill had discovered his spy post, was belly-flat at a point from which he could see a small portion of the rim. And now—that click was returning. Slowly Naill pulled down a straggling branch to form a screen between him and the patroller. With his green skin, his clothing meant to be camouflage in the forest, he believed he did not have to fear detection from above as long as he remained quiet.

It came into view and Naill stared unbelievingly. This was no monster from Janusan past, no alien nightmare. It was something he had seen before—many times! And yet, when his first bewilderment had vanished, he was conscious of small details that were wrong. Before he could count to ten the sentry had vanished past Naill's vision point.

A space-suited off-worlder—walking with the jerky gait of anyone enclosed in the cumbersome covering, the clicking sound coming from the magnetic plates set in the boot soles—an off-worlder in the common rig from any star ship. And yet there were differences about that suit. The whole thing was heavier, with more bulk. And the helmet had the Fors-Genild cocklike hump at the back of the neck. The Fors-Genild had been replaced years ago. Naill tried to remember back to the days when he had had free range of his father's ship. They had had Hammackers on every suit. Why, you only saw the Fors-Genilds now in museum collections of outmoded equipment. That suit could be a hundred years old!

He had to be sure—know that this was not some hallucination induced by the sun and his own faulty day-sight. Naill remained where he was, listening eagerly for the return click of those boots on the rock, thinking furiously. Why would the patroller be wearing a space suit on a planet where all conditions were favorable for his life form— because that was the suit of a Terran, or Terran-descended, explorer.

Click—click...Naill raised his head, as far as he could without moving out from behind his brush screen. Fors-Genild all right! And now that his attention was drawn to that anachronism, he spotted others. The suit *was* old! No modern planet hopper, no matter how out of funds, would entrust his life to a suit from that far in the past. Why, he would not be able to service it, perhaps not even be able to operate some of its archaic equipment.

Which meant...?

Chilled inside in spite of the heat that reached him, Naill waited until those clicks grew fainter and then wriggled back into the tree trunk.

"What is it?" Ashla asked.

Naill hesitated. Oddly enough, he could accept in part that flying thing which was the tool of a reaching alien intelligence. He could accept his own physical change, the presence of Ayyar memory to share his mind, better than he could accept the fact that a hundred-year-old space suit was methodically tramping about the edge of a gully in this wasteland. Was it because the powers of the Iftin *were* alien and so could be accepted as a believing child could accept the wonders of an old tale—while science was represented by that marching suit—an object which was concrete and did not deal with memories or emotions but with stark fact—and here that fact was...wrong?

The suit marched—but what marched inside it? Naill had not been able from where he lay to distinguish any features behind the faceplate of the helmet. All at once he had an odd and completely disturbing vision of an unoccupied suit, animated by what could not be seen or felt, but which obeyed as the flying thing had obeyed.

"What is it?" Ashla crept to his side, her hand on his good shoulder. "What did you see?"

"A space suit—marching." Naill supplied the truth.

"A space suit.... Who?"

Naill shook his head. "What?" he corrected. "It is an old suit, very old."

"Old? They reported once that a hunting party from the port had been lost...."

"Old. No hunter would wear a space suit, no crewman would have to wear one on Janus. This is an Arth planet, entirely suitable for Terran-descended life forms."

"I do not understand."

"I do—in part," Naill told her. "That which is here...has another servant—once off-world, but now his...or its."

"In two hours the sun will be gone." Ashla looked out of the tree trunk, measuring the planet shadows as they lay on the ground. "In the dusk we shall be the favored ones. That suit—it will be clumsy. What wears it cannot move fast across broken ground."

"True." Naill had already made that deduction. But he knew something else—that there was an arms belt about that stalking figure. If not a blaster, it wore tools that could be used as weapons. And he told her so.

"It is very old. Would the charges in the seamer, in the coilcut, still be active?"

Again Naill was surprised by her familiarity with off-world machines and tools.

"I was at the port for a double handful of days after my mother died. There was much to see—to keep one from thinking," she said, answering his unspoken question. "There was no one there to say such learning was evil."

"You had always this liking for worldly knowledge?"

"After the port—yes. Just as I wanted to know more of the forest—not to destroy, as was garth way, but to know it as it is, free and tall and beautiful. Before I was Illylle I had such longings. But that has nothing to do with this space suit and what it may do. I do not believe we can outwait it here."

"No." Naill had already determined that. "Our water is gone, and food. We move with darkness. And perhaps we can do it in this fashion. The gully is long and narrow, running roughly northeast by southwest—or so I remember it when we came in, though I was not too clearheaded." He made a question of that and she closed her eyes, as if better to visualize the territory.

"You are right. And the other end is very narrow—like a sword blade pointed so." She sketched with her fingers.

"If that narrow end can be climbed, it is our best try for a way out. The suit marches at a regular pace. We must creep under cover down the ravine as soon as the dusk is heavy enough, wait for it to be at this end, and then make our break to the west, using every shadow we can for cover."

"There are many chances in that."

"We take them, or sit here until we die or they dig us out like Jamob rats!" Naill snapped.

To his surprise Ashla laughed softly. "Ho, warrior, I do not question the rightness of your plan—for to my mind also it is the only one. But have we the fleetness of foot, the skill in hide-and-seek to bring us out of here?"

"That we shall see." For all his hopes, that statement did not sound as hearty as he wished. And as the long minutes crawled by while they waited for the coming of dusk, Naill experienced first a crowding impatience, and then a growing sense of the utter folly of what they must attempt. By counting his pulse beats he could gauge the pace of the space-suited sentry, judge how long it took the patroller to make the circuit of their ravine. Ashla lay down again, her head pillowed on her arm. Naill wondered, with a small amazement, if she were able to sleep now.

The sunshine could not last forever. Shadows grew, met, spun webs across the valley. And still the click-click of that patrol sounded regularly. At length Naill gave the girl a small shake so she looked up at him.

"We go. But keep down, well under the bushes. And do not touch any plants if you can help."

"You mean the eaters. Yes, I have seen what they do. But they are closing with the dark. Take care of your arm. Shall I re-sling it for you?"

"No, it is better at my side if we must crawl. Now—keep behind me and do not move the brush if you can help it."

It was one of those periods when every minute spun into an hour of listening, of movement kept agonizingly to a minimum. Naill longed to get to his feet, to run for the sword-point end of the valley in leaping bounds, yet he must make a lizard's sly

passage. They cowered together, halfway down
the length of their way, as the suit stamped by
above. And again when only a quarter of their
journey still lay ahead, as it passed on the other
side.

Then they reached the point, facing a narrow
crevice. Ten feet above—maybe a little more—the
open rock of the waste plain would lie open. To get
straight back to the river would mean passing the
patroller in the open, and that Naill dared not try
unless he was left no other choice.

"Now!" He started up the crevice, praying no
slide would start from the clutch of his fingers, the
dig of his booted toes. He pulled himself up,
supported and steadied by the girl below. Then he
lay across the rim and reached down with his good
arm to assist her in turn.

They could see the sentry almost halfway down
the right side of its return journey.

"To the left!" Thankfully Naill sighted an inky
blot of shadow cast by a standing spar of rock.

It was the sword that betrayed them. Naill had
set it back into the sheath before he had climbed.
But now, as he moved, weapon and scabbard
scraped the stone and the noise was loud.

"Quick!" Ashla caught at him, pulled him on.
"Oh, please—quick!"

Somehow they made it, to sprawl into that patch
of dark. But the regular click-click of the space
boots had become a rat-tat. Then—silence. Was the
patroller readying one of the weapon tools from its
suit belt? Would a lash of flame, meant to seal a

break of ship skin, cut across their rock as a herdsman would use a stock whip to snap straying animals back to the herd?

"Ayyar—behind you!"

Naill twisted about.

No space suit marched from that side. These were pallid, leaping, moving things—resembling the hounds of the garths and yet unlike. For the hounds were animals, and their kind had long been subservient and known by mankind. While these were of another breed, outside all natural laws Naill understood.

"The Larsh wytes!"

Now Ayyar remembered—remembered such packs, hunting among the trees of Iftcan. That had been an ill hunting but one he had faced, sword ready, as he did now.

A narrow head with eyes that were sparks of sun, blasting yellow, snapped at him and he swung at it, to cleave skull, tumble the pack leader back among its fellows. There was no time to choose his next kill for bared teeth were reaching for his throat. Naill stabbed upwards, saw another of the wytes fall.

"Behind me!" he ordered Ashla.

"Not so! I, too, hunt wytes this night!" he heard her cry in return. He saw her use the long hunting knife to cover them from a rush on the left.

Their surprise attack a costly failure, the pack withdrew a little. One at the rear raised its head to voice a long howl. From the dark sky came an answer...the cry of the flying thing which had earlier hung above the gully. And then, while the wytes held them fast to their rock spire, the suited sentry strode into view.

They were strange partners, the wytes and the metal-enclosed unknown. But the wytes accepted the suited figure as their leader, drawing aside to let it pass. It stalked into a space directly before the fugitives and stood there. Naill tried desperately to see the face behind the helmet plate. The once-clear surface of that section was fogged, webbed by a maze of fine cracks and lines, completely masking its wearer.

"Watch—oh, watch!"

He had been so intent upon trying to learn the identity of their foe that he had not seen that movement of the gloved hands until Ashla called out.

But no warning could have saved them, Naill knew. The early suit might be clumsy according to modern standards. But it had been of the best engineering and design of its time, equipped for dangerous and demanding duty. Once that small object now spinning at them had been set and dispatched, nothing short of a blaster would deter it from completing its mission.

They were not going to be flamed out of existence. They were to be the helpless captives of what wore that suit, hid behind the cracked faceplate—or its master!

FIFTEEN   THE WHITE FOREST

A shallow bowl of valley stretched on down and away from where they had paused. And the reaching moonlight made a shimmering maze of glinting, prismatic light there. Naill shielded his eyes with his good hand. Ashla's fingers closed on his arm.

"The White Forest...." Her voice was emotionless, drained, and not, he thought, by the fatigue of their journey over the broken plain of the waste.

Since that throw ray had circled them back at the edge of this forbidden territory, they had marched straight on northward into the unknown, their space-suited captor in the lead, the pack of wytes padding at a distance but covering the rear—a weird assortment of travelers.

The ray had kept them docile enough, made them move in answer to the projected command of whatever lurked within the suit. And there had been no answer to all their attempts to communicate with that. Was their goal this forest?

For forest it was, if one judged that term applied to growths that arose vertically into the air from grounded roots, spread branches, grouped closely together. But this was a forest of branching, glittering crystals. No leaves rustled here, no color save the rainbow flickers that twinkled and sparkled in the moonlight. It was as if ice had chosen to reproduce trees and had succeeded in part.

The ray control pulled them on, downslope, into that place of cold and deadly beauty. Because deadly it was. Ayyar memory in Naill brought fear, the terror known when a man faces something far greater than himself as an enemy—not personally, but to all his species. As early men of the Terran breed had feared the dark and what might walk in that blackness their eyes could not pierce, so did the Iftin-born hold an age-old aversion to stark light and what could dwell comfortably in its glare. But Naill and Ashla had no choice—there was no breaking that invisible pull between them and the space suit stalking forward, towing them as a man might tow a recalcitrant hound.

As they were drawn over the lip, down into that

place of white light, the wytes no longer dogged them. Perhaps they, too, found this a place of terror and did not have to brave that terror.

Naill's boots crunched on a surface that gave in brittle fashion beneath his weight. He glanced down, saw that there was a trail of broken crystals powdered into sparkling dust. The ponderous footfalls of the suited guard were clearly marked, lying over other tracks—perhaps many of them.

Now there was another sound or sounds—a tinkling, coming from the growths or pillars making up the forest. As they drew closer, Naill could see that those horizontally branching shafts stood tall, not with the overwhelming height of the tree towers of Iftcan, but tall indeed compared to his own inches.

"The White Forest," Ashla repeated. "Tall it grows, straight it stands." Her voice held the queer singing note which Naill had come to associate with Illylle speaking through changeling lips. "But it is not real—it does not live. . . . Therefore—it is not!"

What she meant he did not understand, but oddly enough her denial of what they could both see was a lift to his spirits.

"Built—grown by a will," she continued. "It lives by a will, it will die by a will. But this will cannot make another Iftcan, no matter how it tries."

They had passed under the wide, stiffly held branches of the first "tree," and her words returned as faint, whispering echoes. The chiming tinkle grew stronger, a hiss of answering anger.

Ashla laughed. Her hand lifted to point a slim green finger at the next tree.

"Grow leaves—but you cannot! Nourish life—but you cannot! Shade the traveler—but you cannot! Feed with your fruits—but you cannot! Bend to the storm—but you cannot! Forest which is no true forest—beware the life, the storm, that which you have not...." Her voice sank again, and once more her hand reached for and clasped Naill's.

"Why did I say that?" she asked. "If I could only hold the old knowledge in my head as you hold the sword in your hand—then perhaps together we might follow the path of Kymon and—and..." She shook her head. "Even the manner of the triumph of Kymon is lost to me now. Only, I tell you, Naill-Ayyar, that had we the old knowledge we could fight. There is a secret that slips through my memory when I would have it forth.... Always it is just gone from me. This is a place of Power, but not the Power of Iftcan—and therefore one Power might be ranged against the other, had we only the proper key."

The hissing tinkle of the forest waxed stronger, making an odd rustling which lapped them about. But there was no change in the pace of the suit, drawing them after it in the grip of the ray-hold.

The faint path, which had wound down the slope, now led in a curling curve among the boles of the crystal trees, while the moonlight reflected and re-reflected on glittering nobs and surfaces confused and bewildered. If the lesser light of the moon proved so formidable, what would sunlight make of this mirror-trunked forest?

There was no evidence of any native life. As Ashla had accused, this was a dead place, dead without ever having held life as they knew it.

"Does Illylle remember this?" Naill appealed to the girl by his side.

"A little—far too little."

"Any idea where we may be going?" he persisted.

"No—save that it will be a place where there is peril, for this is the opposite of that which dwells in the Mirror—it balances this against that as a harvest is weighed on the Speaker's scales."

The ground still sloped down. Naill had not been able to judge during their short halt on the rim of the valley how large a territory the crystal erections covered. Perhaps whatever controlled the space-suited sentry, the wytes—the flying thing—lay in the very heart of this land.

Naill's mouth was dry; his ankle ached dully as did his arm. And he knew that Ashla must be as hungry, tired, and thirsty as he was. Food, water, a chance to rest—they needed those badly, might need them more before this journey came to an end.

Above their heads the crystal branches wove a crisscross net shutting out the night sky. They were capped over by an icy cover. Could they some way mark a trail against a possible retreat?

Naill was shocked out of that speculation by Ashla's fingers biting deep into his flesh in a convulsive grip. Startled, he looked around, but her eyes were not for him. Her gaze was fixed on a tree ahead and to the left.

"Look!" The merest whisper directed him.

Naill obeyed. By some trick of the reflecting surfaces there was a mirror of sorts. And pictured on it...

At first he thought that greenish figure was himself—or Ashla. Then he knew that at such an angle their own reflections would be impossible. No—that was an Ift, but a stranger! Who? And where?

They were pulled ahead two steps and that shadow image was gone, vanished as if it had never been at all. But they were left with the knowledge that they were not alone in this glittering prison.

If what or whoever walked in the space suit had seen that momentary reflection, there was no hint of it, no pause in the steady pace it set. Almost Naill could persuade himself that he had seen nothing either, but Ashla held to its reality.

"An Ift—one of us," she told him softly. "Another prisoner."

"How can you be sure of that?"

"Because—an Ift in the White Forest could only be a prisoner. To us this place is death!"

Their captor crunched on, and the invisible tow cord on which he held both of them continued its unrelenting pull. The ground now leveled out. They must be at the foot of the valley wall, close to its heart and whatever secret it did hold. Here the crystal trees stood very tall, approaching the lower "towers" of Iftcan in size. And for much of their length their trunks were unbroken by branches. Those bare limbs existed close to their crown, forming a roof overhead, but leaving much space underneath.

Abruptly the prisoners were at the head of a stairway, much like the stairs that had led up to the mountain-cupped Mirror, but which here reached downward into a second valley or crevice bitten sharply into the earth, as if some giant warrior had struck with a sword blade to divide a furrow in soft and yielding soil. Yet here was no soil...the ground itself had a glassy glaze that struck back at their eyes with punishing light.

Naill surveyed that stair with foreboding. The acute angle of descent would tax a strong man. He doubted if the two of them could make it now. For the first time since it had taken them captive and turned to march into this wilderness, the space-suited leader made a move other than just walking. Its metal-mittened hands arose to chest level, and it cast from it, with a lazy toss, a small disk.

Ashla screamed and Naill shouted. They were whipped after that spinning disk, their feet skidding and slipping on the slick surface of that glassy verge, pulled on out into the air above the crevice—with no hope of escape.

But a swift plunge to ghastly oblivion did not follow as Naill expected. Though their feet had left the surface of the ground and they lay extended forward on what he would swear was air alone, they were not falling—they were floating, as a man might in the free fall of a spaceship, descending into the gulf, that was true, but not at a speed to crush them when they met the surface below.

The walls rising about them were cream-white, smooth save for that ribbon of stairway. Naill spun his body around with memories of how it had once been on board ship. However, when he tried to move closer to Ashla, or "swim" toward the wall stairway, he was still under inhibiting control.

Ashla was quiet after her first scream of fear, but Naill could hear her breathing heavily, see that her eyes were wide open, her features setting in a mask of naked terror. She had had no defense against the strangeness of this, no memory of free fall in space to sustain her.

"This—is—free—fall—as—on—a ship," Naill got out. His outflung hand closed about her wrist, so that their bodies drew a little closer together. "This is controlled—perhaps by the ray disk."

It was where they were going, not how, that mattered now. Below them, all he could see was a murky billowing, darker than the walls, as if some fire steamed or smoked there. Yet there was no warmth in the air. As the first streamers of that murk engulfed them, Naill felt no change in temperature. His initial nightmare faded; they were not being wafted down into a furnace.

The murk grew thicker. He kept his hold on Ashla. Close as they now were, it was difficult to distinguish her features. They were as blind here as they would have been in broad sunlight, if for a different reason. How long had they fallen? Naill had tried to keep count of the steps in that stair but knew that he had missed out long since. And still they continued to float down. Then, breaking through the fog, came more formations of crystal. Unlike the trees of the upper forest, these appeared in clusters of roughly geometric shape—they could be towers, ramparts, the bulk of alien buildings—while through them ran small pulsing lines of light, to no pattern Naill could perceive, save that they formed veins in the surfaces, as the veins carrying the blood to serve his own body.

There was a bright flash of light at their feet while they were still above the surface of the ground. Whatever sustained them vanished in that wink, and they fell in a rush, landing in an angle between two of the now towering crystalline walls.

Naill sat up, pulling Ashla with him. The tinkling bell which had become a part of the world since they had entered the White Forest was silenced. They had ceased to note it consciously while they heard it, but the quiet that followed was so complete it awed them both.

"What is this place?" Ashla held tight to Naill, did not try to move.

"Illylle does not know?" He appealed for some scrap of memory to aid them now.

She shook her head. "Illylle sleeps—or is gone." There was a desolation of loneliness in her answer.

Naill strove to make his own contact. There was no touching any point of Ayyar memory. They were totally on their own, intruders, prisoners in an alien place. But that fact was no reason to sit and await trouble! One could choose a battlefield. And he had an idea that when the ray control had hit ground, it had broken, that they were now free of its bounds.

"Come!" He pulled her to her feet. His left arm in its splints was still fastened to his side as he had had her do before they set out. He would leave it so. At least he could use his right, and the sword he had sheathed after their capture by the ray had been left him by the space-suited enemy. What defense that blade could be against the intelligence responsible for their present plight Naill did not know. But the hilt felt good to his hand when his palm closed about it.

"Where would you go?" Ashla asked.

Her question was a just one. The fog swirled about the crystal walls, leaked through apertures in them. There was no visibility for more than a few yards in any direction. On the other hand every instinct in Naill warred against remaining where the disk had landed them. If the fog was a hindrance it might also be a help, giving them cover. He said as much.

"Which way, then?" Ashla did not protest, but turned as she stood, studying the hardly visible landscape.

"As we fell—that stairway was over there." Naill pointed. "Perhaps we can reach its foot."

"And is there also a chance of finding food"— her tongue ran over her dry, cracking lips—"and water?"

"I do not know."

"There is this, we were brought here carefully. Had our deaths been planned, what need to spare us that fall?" Ashla spoke slowly as if reasoning it out in her own mind. "So—"

"So—somewhere here is food and water? You may be right, but the price of wasting time in a blind search..."

"While one lives, there is always a chance. If we climb the stair, we only come out in the forest once again...to find that suited thing waiting—or the sun up! And the sun shining in there!"

She did not need to elaborate. To climb into sunlight blazing on those crystal trees would be climbing into sure death for Iftin bodies—even if they could drag their way up that long stairway.

"Which way, then?" Naill asked in turn.

"This is a time when perhaps we must depend upon chance." Ashla stooped to pick up an object she tossed from hand to hand. "This is what brought us here—let us see if, by the whims of chance, it can take us even farther!" She shut her eyes and turned rapidly around before she threw the disk from her.

There was a faint tinkle and they both saw the disk rebound from a wall to lie on the earth in an opening. It was an illogical and reckless way to decide their next move, but Naill accepted it. Together they went through the doorway.

It was a gate rather than a doorway, for the space beyond was as open to the air overhead as that where they had landed. This was a corridor of sorts running straight ahead. Walls of crystal stood higher than their heads, half curtained by the mist.

"Listen!" Perhaps some trick of those crystal-line walls carried and magnified that sound. Ashla was already hurrying toward that unmistakable murmur of water.

They sped down that hallway, and the sound of the water grew stronger as they stumbled eagerly along. There was another doorway, and they came through it to a space Naill believed to be truly open, though he could see little of its area. Ashla sprang on.

"This way! Over here!"

What they came upon was no natural river as they had known before. Water flowed there right enough, but it swirled at a race through a trough of crystal.

"Wait—!" A remnant of Ayyar's hunter's caution made Naill call out.

She did not listen to him. Falling to her knees, Ashla plunged both hands into the flood. She might have been testing the validity of what her eyes reported. Then, the water running down her arms, she made a cup of her fingers and drank.

It might be the wildest kind of folly to trust the wholesomeness of what they found there. But Naill's resistance was swept away. He followed her example, and the moisture on his skin, the liquid he splashed one-handed into his dry mouth, smelled no different, tasted no different, from any that he had drunk from forest springs and pools. It was cold, clear—like new life flowing into his whole body.

"You see"—Ashla smiled—"in this much, chance favored us. We have found water."

Naill sat back on his heels, his first craving satisfied. "We may have found more than water." Now his wits were working again, weighing every small point that might operate in their favor.

"How?"

"The water comes—and it goes...."

"You mean—follow this stream to its source or its end? Yes, that is good—very good!"

"The water makes a good guide, a better one than any other we have seen here. And we have no means of carrying a drinking supply if we do leave it." He had been forced to abandon the remains of his pack, with its water bottle and food back by the river.

"Guide and sustainer all in one. But which way do we go—upstream or down?"

Naill could see small difference in choice. Either way could serve their purpose. But before he could say that, Ashla gave a little cry and leaned out over the trough, her hand flashing down into the water, coming up with something in its grasp.

What she held was a fussan pod, empty of seed, but still fresh.

"Upstream! This came from upstream. Where there is one there may be more!"

Naill's hopes arose with hers. He got stiffly to his feet, favoring his aching arm. "Upstream it is—let us go!"

"I thought"—Ashla's tongue caressed her lips—
"that I would long for nothing as much as I wished
for water. But now I find hunger can also be a pain.
And one cannot eat crystal. Is there no end to this
stream or this place?"

"It looks as if we are coming to something now."
Naill had been striving to pierce the fog-mist, and
the vague outline he had seen though its swirls
appeared to remain firm in spite of the coming and
going of that tenuous curtain.

What lay before them was a wall of crystal,
stretching, as far as they could tell, clear across the
valley. And the water guide which had led them

there poured in a rush through a conduit in that wall far too small to provide an entrance to whatever space lay beyond. Ashla dropped down limply.

"I cannot go back. I am sorry, but I cannot go back." She said that simply, her sober tone underlining her surrender to this last blow.

"Not back!" Naill went directly to the wall. The crystal was not smooth but studded with irregularities, pocked with hollows. This could be climbed—not by a one-handed man, perhaps, but Ashla might do it. "Not back," he reiterated firmly, "but over! This is as rough as a ladder."

She was drawn by his confidence to approach the wall. Then she glanced at him.

"And you? Do you sprout wings to bear you over?"

"No—but there is this." Naill unslung the sword shoulder belt. "If you get to the top, hook this about one of those large projections. Then I will have a hand hold to bring me up in turn."

Ashla regarded first the wall and then Naill doubtfully. He strove to break through her hesitancy.

"We must do it now—while we still have a measure of strength in us. Or do you wish to remain here bewailing our fate until hunger is a finish?"

To his surprise Ashla smiled at that, a stretch of her too thin face which lacked any real pleasure but held a haunting suggestion of wistfulness.

"As you point out, warrior, struggle is always better than surrender. I shall climb."

Privately Naill was not sure that even with the aid of the belt he could make it. But this was their only chance. Judging by his own swimming head and weakened body, he was certain she was right; they could not now retrace their road down the valley.

Ashla climbed slowly and with caution, testing each hold before she entrusted her full weight to it. It seemed to Naill that the minutes of that climb lengthened into hours. Then her head and shoulders topped the edge of the wall and she was able to see over. Seconds later, her face alight and eager, she looked down at him.

"We were right! Here is true forest! We were right!"

Her report provided him with a last spurt of strength, enough to give him the necessary energy to reach the perch on which she now clung, her hands and the dangling belt at his service. Then they steadied one another as they gazed out over a section of welcoming gray-green, full of beckoning shadows. This was not Iftcan—it was not even the forest upon which the settlers preyed—but it was far closer to it than any land they had seen since they had entered the waste by the river.

Naill was not wholly conscious of anything save that green. Then the sudden rigidity of Ashla's body against his own broke his absorption.

The girl's head stretched forward on her shoulders. Her pointed ears flared wide from her skull, and her eyes were fixed in a probing stare on the forest before them.

"What is it?" Naill's first surge of relief was erased by a thrust of alarm. He heard nothing, saw not even a leaf tremble in that waiting woodland. "Tell me—what is it?"

But he was too late. Ashla had already moved, swinging over the barrier on the far side, descending by a series of reckless holds and half falls that frightened him. Then, without a single backward glance—as if he had ceased to exist for her—she ran on across the small strip of powdered crystal sand to the trees and disappeared among them as if a green mouth had gulped her in.

"Ashla! Illylle!" Naill's voice rang hollowly, a lonesome sound deadened and swallowed into a thin echo by some sonic property of this place. He dared not move as fast as she had. His descent was slow and clumsy, but at last he did reach the ground.

From this level the greenery ahead had a solid, forbidding look. Naill studied what he could see of it. Here, too, the mists trailed, one moment hiding, the next revealing a section. But this was true forest growth, he thought. And—Ashla had already gone that way. He strode over the small traces left by her running feet on the sand.

Outwardly this was the same forest as that beyond the crystal growth to the east. His ears now picked up the small muted sounds of insects and other life within its hold. Muted—that was it! This place was shadowed, reduced, in a fashion Naill could not define, from the life of the other woods he had walked.

His hunter's eyes followed the signs of Ashla's

headlong passage—snapped twigs, torn leaves, the print of her boots in the soil. She must have burst on as if striving to reach some goal with no care for any obstacles in between. Why? Just another of those endless questions that were a part of this world.

Naill used the sword to beat and cut himself passage in the same direction the girl had taken. Then the point of that blade struck into the open, and he followed it—into a clearing.

Two—three—four of them, counting the one who faced Ashla. Four green-skinned, large-eared—changelings? Or Iftin of the true blood? They were all men, clad in ragged remains of the same forest dress as Naill had found in Iftsiga. Two of them wore shoulder-belted swords like his own. One had a wooden spear headed with a crystal point. Naill took that in, in a quick evaluation of the company.

Then the man before Ashla drew his full regard and, studying him, Naill forgot the rest.

The stranger was perhaps by an inch or so the tallest of the group, but he was not otherwise physically outstanding. It was . . . Naill tried to be objective, tried to understand why, when looking at this ragged, quiet man, he was moved to respect, ready to surrender some of his independence and will. There was only a moment of such desire before Naill fought it down.

"Who are you?" The man spoke and Naill was about to reply when he realized the question was not addressed to him but to Ashla.

"Illylle—and you are Jarvas." She spoke with

conviction, almost impatiently as one who found such a question stupid and unnecessary.

The man's hand came up in a gesture of warning, as if to ward off her words. "I am Pate Sissions."

"You are Jarvas—Mirrormaster!"

He moved then, swiftly. His hand clapped over her mouth, his right arm crushed her into captivity. Naill leaped out with ready sword.

Ashla's struggles pulled her captor about as she fought wildly against his hold, useless as that was. They staggered together and Naill hesitated, afraid to strike Ashla. That hesitation was his own undoing. His instinct warned a fraction of a second too late. The wooden butt of the spear struck against the side of his head, sending him down.

Cool...green.... He lay on moss in Iftcan, and above him boughs made an autumn wind sing. Tonight there would be the Festival of Leaf Farewell and he would go into the Court of the Maidens for the choosing.

Maidens—one maiden...a thin face, wan, always a little tired and sad, Ashla—no, Illylle! Illylle—Ashla, name balanced name. Ashla was Illylle, Illylle Ashla.

"So—it is thus, little sister. Here we are as we were—and so we must remain until we win forth."

Words out of the air. Naill made no sense of them. But he heard in answer, "I am Ashla—of the garths, then."

"You are Ashla always—here. Do not forget it. And I am Pate, and this is Monro, and Derek, and

Torry. And your impetuous young friend is Naill. We are off-worlders and settlers—no more, never any more than that."

"But we are not. Just a look at us would seal that truth."

"We are totally alien to this Power. It is the mind, the memory that mind holds, not the physical form that matters to it. Now It is doubtful, still uncertain concerning our identity. Once It learns the truth—"

"I understand."

Naill knew that he did not. But he forced open his eyes, turned his head. He lay on a mat of leaves under a rough lean-to, looking out at a small fire around which sat the four men and Ashla. The man beside her turned his head, his eyes found Naill. He arose lithely and came to kneel beside the other.

"How do you feel?"

"Who are you?" Naill countered.

"I am Pate Sissions—First-In Scout of Survey. And"—his hand gestured to the company by the fire—"that is Haf Monro, astropilot of the *Thorstone*."

Distant memory stirred in Naill. *Thorstone*—a long-lost cruiser by that name...what *was* the story?

"Derek Versters of Versters' Garth, and Ladim Torry, medico of the Karbon Combine."

Karbon Combine? But the Karbon people had been off Janus for almost a full generation! Yet the outwardly green-skinned Ift whom Sissions had so introduced appeared to be a man still in his first youth. First-In Scout, astropilot, garthman, Kar-bon medico—a wide range of occupations on Janus, covering perhaps the full length of time the planet had been known to Survey.

"You are all"—Naill broke out the word he had first heard back at Kosburg's—"changelings!"

Sissions' big-eared head swung slowly from left to right in gesture of negation made more impress-ibe by the very length of that movement.

"We are off-worlders—from different times and worlds—who came to Janus for different reasons. That is what we are—and will be—*here*. And you are?"

"Naill Renfro—bought laborer."

"Good enough. Continue to remember that, Naill Renfro, and we shall deal easily together. Sorry we had to knock you out—there was not time to reason with you."

"Where is this place? And how did you get here?" Naill pulled himself up to rest on the elbow of his right arm. His head was thick and ached dully, but he was not so dim-witted now as not to realize that there was a method in Sissions' speech, that he had been warned against some very real danger.

"As to this place—well, it is a prison of sorts." Sissions sat down cross-legged. "We are not sure ourselves as to the reason for our detention here. Except that it means trouble. How did we get here? Well, we came in various ways at different times. Monro and I were hunting a friend who had come in this direction and vanished. We were picked up—"

"By an animated space suit?" Naill cut in.

"By a walking space suit," Sissions agreed. "We found Torry here already—he was first in residence. They caught him near the river where he tried to take a shortcut west. And Derek—Derek came later with a companion who chose to leave."

"You can leave?" Naill demanded in surprise.

"You can leave, provided you are intent upon committing suicide. An agile man with a great amount of determination and no sense can climb to the White Forest. Whether he can get through there..." Sissions shrugged.

"So you just sit around and wait for what is going to happen?" Naill's amazement grew. His whole reading of this man suggested that such a spineless course was so alien to his nature that Naill could not believe Sissions was in earnest.

"So we wait," Sissions assured him. "We wait, and we remember who and what we are."

Again that inflection of warning. Naill sat all the way up. They were watching him with a kind of detached inspection, as if waiting for him to make some move by which they would then be influenced into an important judgment and appraisal.

"How long do we wait?" he asked quietly.

"We do not know. Perhaps until the opposition moves so we can learn who—or what—It really is. Or until we find our own solution. Now—" Sissions piked up a small bowl, handed it to Naill. Through the substance of the container he felt the warmth of the contents. Eagerly he savored and then gulped the stew.

"Light coming." Torry stood up, the crystal-pointed spear in his hand. "Best back to the burrow." He came to Naill and together with Sissions assisted him to his feet.

"Where are we going?"

"Out of the sun," the former medico told him shortly. "In the day period here we're as good as blind. To be caught in the open is bad."

"To be caught in the White Forest in the sun," Sissions added, "that's the end. And we've not been able to work out any way of crossing that in one night's time. That is the lock on our prison cell, Renfro."

Naill could see the right in that reasoning. The crystal forest in the moonlight had been hard enough to face. Its brilliance under direct sunshine would burn out their night-oriented sight.

"There was one of our kind up there when we came in—we saw his reflection on a tree," he reported.

"Halsfad!" Derek pushed closer. "Where? How near the edge of the forest was he? Pate—maybe he was able to make it after all!"

"We could not tell," Naill replied. "The reflections must be deceiving."

Sissions agreed. "Could have been from any direction. And even if he reached the edge of the forest before sunup—what then?"

What then indeed? The miles of baked and empty rockland ahead with no shelter—Naill thought of that. Yes, it made an effective prison for all of them. And desperate flight was not the answer; he understood Sissions the better now.

"Home." Monro had been in advance. Now he

stood before a dark hole, folding back a curtain woven of plaited leaves. Ashla crept after him, and they followed one by one until they were all within the shelter.

Its skeleton was a tree with huge exposed roots, roots that extended out of the hole well above their heads as might branches, but running down to the earth, rather than horizontally, so that the center trunk appeared to be supported by a fringe of props. In and out through that grid of exposed roots leaves had been woven, lengths of dried vine, and pieces of bark, to form a structure with the living tree as its center.

Ashla went directly to that trunk and set both of her palms flat against its bark.

> "Iftin wall, Iftin roof,
> Wood lives, wood—"

Even as he had jumped her in the clearing, so was Sissions upon her again, his hand across her lips with the force of a slap.

She raised hers from the tree to twist and tear at his fingers until she had freed her mouth.

"You have forgotten too much!" That was Illylle speaking now with all the force of command she had shown at those times when the Iftin took precedence over the Terran in her. "This is Iftscar—from the true seed. It will not betray us. Though why it should grow in the White Land ...ah!" She nodded, not at them, but at some thought or memory. "When Kymon journeyed forth, with him went a pouch blessed by the

Counters of the Seed, and they gave him of their powers. So—here fell a nut of Iftscar, and through the long time of the True Leaves it has grown. Look into your memory, Jarvas, Mirrormaster that was—you have been too timid by half!"

She turned in his hold, her hands now rising to cup over his eyes. At first Sissions moved under her touch as if to push her away. Then he stiffened, straightened, and slowly—very slowly—his own hands went out to rest against the tree trunk as hers had done before him. Ashla stepped aside and left him so.

"Iftscar!" She flung up her arms in a gesture of welcome. "We shelter here. In the Leaf of the Gray we claim what you have to give us."

"Pate—Pate!" Monro would have dropped hand on Sissions' shoulder, but the girl fended him off.

"Let be! He takes the strength he should have drunk long ago. He forgot when he should have remembered! Let be—you have not the Seeing!"

Sissions' hands fell from the tree trunk. He turned, his eyes wide. Then he blinked and came back from some immeasurable distance.

It was to Ashla he spoke: "I am indeed a fool. There may yet be a key we have not tried, already set in our hands."

"If you had not the right memory then you were wise not to hunt lost keys. Is it not with all of you as it is with Naill and with me—that you possess only parts of memories, but not the full recall of your Iftin selves?"

"Yes."

"And so you fear—and wisely—what you do not

control nor know. I believe, Mirrormaster, that such caution is not folly but wisdom."

"Perhaps two memories knitted well together may supply us with the key to this prison!" Sissions held out both hands to her, and hers fell palm down on his.

Naill watched them with a strange lost feeling. Ayyar—who had been Ayyar after all? A fighting man who at the last testing had gone down to defeat. A simple warrior who dared not use the Mirror of Thanth, but had fled from its challenge. And Naill Renfro—a slave laborer from the Dipple. Neither part of him had been a man of strength or power—perhaps the whole was less...

"Many memories"—Ashla's eyes went from man to man—"but maybe too different. To weave a power there must be unity. We can but try, you who were Jarvas."

"What's going on?" Monro demanded sharply.

"We may have been too cautious." Sissions was again the off-worlder in speech and idiom. "This tree house gives us immunity to certain forces here. Now"—his glance caught them, held them, demanded—"we shall try pooling our Iftin memories, and from such a harvest perhaps we can glean what we need—to tip the scales of fortune on our side."

"But you said—" Derek began and frowned at Ashla. "She appears able to change your mind quickly enough."

"We have never been able to decide whether we have these Iftin memories by plan—or by chance. Perhaps we'll never know the truth of that. But today—for the first time—two of us who had certain powers in our Iftin identities have met. If we can join those powers, draw other knowledge from the rest of you"—Sissions' head was high, his eagerness was in his voice, mirrored on his face—"this can lead us to freedom! We can only try—but are you willing to join?"

There was a hesitancy, but one by one they gave their assent.

Naill's back was against one of the roots of the trees which formed the refuge. He nursed his splinted arm across his knee. And thought.

They had carried out Ashla's suggestion, pooled their Iftin memories, only to discover that those memories were so diverse that they had little common meeting ground. Their Ift personalities appeared to have come not only from various places but also from eras well separated in time. So they had found no key to their prison.

One would need the protection of a space suit to travel the White Forest and its surrounding waste by day. And they could not hope to make that journey in a single night starting from this site.

Space suit.... Naill battened down all Iftin memories and strove to recall those of Naill Renfro—a very young Naill Renfro. He had been what—six? seven? eight?—when the *Lydian Lady* had been caught in the orbital battle about Calors. Spaceborn and bred, he realized that planet time did not count much in his early days. And what did he know of space suits?

He had had one, made to his size, and he could remember how the instruction in its use had come by hyposleep. Twice he had worn it, going out with his father on one heat-baked, desert planet, and again when taken on a tour of the outer hull of the ship as part of his space training and discipline. Yes, he could recall that without difficulty—everything about the suit, its handling, servicing and equipment.

The point was that now there was a suit out there, mobile, in use—in use by something non-Terran, which might make all the difference. Even if they could not take that suit—and capture what used it—a suit meant a ship somewhere. And Naill was certain that no off-worlder had deliberately wandered far from a ship in that cumbersome rig, not all the way from the present spaceport—that was certain.

Item two was that this waste and what governed it was unknown at the port. And he had heard nothing concerning it from the settlers. None of those prisoners here had been taken until they crossed into the waste. Whatever ruled here did not venture forth to seek prey; it waited for it to come within short reach.

Therefore—the space suit meant a ship not too far away. And to Naill a ship meant a possible supply of weapons, a hope of defense and offense. Let Ashla and Sissions try to use Iftin methods against the enemy—that never-defined enemy! There might be another way altogether!

However, if there was, surely the men here had already searched for it. Sissions claimed to be a First-In Scout. Those explorers of Survey were noted for their elasticity of thinking, ability to improvise and experiment. And Monro was an astro-navigator whose attention would be centered on ships. They could not or would not have overlooked the connection between space suit and ship here.

Yet the thought of those two—suit and ship— continued to work in his mind. Naill brought up all the old arguments—that such a ship, did it exist nearby, could long ago have been stripped. The suit was an old model, very old.

"How's the arm?" Naill was shaken out of his thoughts as Torry knelt beside him. "Any pain?"

"An ache now and then." Naill realized that he had not felt much discomfort for some time now. The arm, stiffly bound and splinted, was a cumbersome nuisance, but otherwise it did not bother him too much.

"Let me take a look. You know—we all heal more quickly since we changed our skins. We're tougher in many ways. I wish I knew more about what happened to us...."

"You're from the port, aren't you?" Naill asked. "How did you get the Green Sick?"

"The same way we were all suckered in—because I was curious. I went out on a field trip—trying to pick up some native plants to study. I found one of the treasure caches, came down sick before I could rejoin my party. As far as I knew, I might have something highly contagious—so I kept clear. Then it was too late—I was changed and I didn't want to go back."

"What's the purpose of the caches, the changes?" Naill watched the other skillfully unwrap and unsplint his arm.

"Any pain?" Fingers ran along his skin, exerting pressure.

"No."

"I'd say that had knitted true. Favor it a bit, but you can leave off the rest of this. The purpose of the caches? Just what you've seen—to gain recruits."

"For whom and what?"

"None of us really know; we have only a general idea. Sissions was the first capture. And he's helped with the recruiting ever since. We have a compulsion at certain times of the year to set those traps; we can't help ourselves. As far as we can make out, there was a civilization native to Janus a long time ago. They worked with nature, did not seek to oppose or control her. No machines for them. There came a time when that race went into decline—finally they were overrun and wiped out."

"By the Larsh!" Naill cut in. "I remember!"

"Do you? Derek does too, but Pate and I and Monro don't—we're all from an earlier period.

Anyway, after the fall of Iftcan there could only
have been a handful of survivors. But that handful
appears to have numbered among them some of
their scientists. They must have developed the
treasure chests then, planted a few to wait. They
certainly had hope, or trust, or some inkling that
another race would arise here, or come from space,
to trigger those installations. Anyone who does
handle cache things—with liking—assumes the
personality and body changes connected with that
particular cache. To this day *we* don't know how
they work. But there has to be some bond of
sympathy between the finder and one of the
objects included in that collection."

"But if Pate Sissions was the First-In Scout of
Survey, then he must have landed here—" Naill
stared at Torry.

"About a hundred and twenty planet years
ago?" Torry nodded. "Yes."

"But he's—he's a young man!" Naill countered.

"We have no idea of the life span of the original
Iftin, or what happened to our bodies during the
Green Sick. As far as we can tell, after the change
there is very little aging for us. I have been this
way for nearly seventy-five planet years. But our
numbers grow very slowly, since not all caches are
found—and some take no captives."

Naill tried to digest the thought of agelessness.
He was not unaware that some alien races had
achieved life spans far beyond that of the Terran
breed. But how could such a change be wrought in
a Terran body?

"The caches can attract only certain types,"

Torry continued. "And the method of selection and control of such captives is another secret we have not broken. We number now only a few more than a hundred—just thirty of them women. Five children have been born—and they are Iftin from the beginning. Also—they have no memories. Still we are bound to set the traps. Sissions and I were here on such a mission when we were taken prisoner."

"You do not live in Iftcan?"

"We have a base there. That is where Pate found the first treasure which started us all along this road. But our new home is west, overseas. Until we learn more, we can only have patience and do what we can to re-establish our kind."

"Until?" Naill asked.

"Until we are again a nation. You know the First Law—a world having an intelligent native population and a civilization can be given a choice; to join the Federation or warn off all contact. In time we shall have Janus—we grow more Iftin with the years. And the off-worlders cannot hold this planet against our will."

"But the settlers—"

"Are not natives. They would change Janus, alter it to an off-world pattern, narrow, arid, and stultifying. They are slowly shrinking in numbers as more and more of them come over to us. This world does not welcome them, and those it can welcome speedily find a cache and join our ranks—as you came, and Ashla. What part of the treasure lured you so that you had to handle it, wanted to possess it for yourself?"

"The tube," Naill replied instantly. "It was the color—those patterns.... Something pulled me—I cannot explain."

"For me it was the figurine." Torry smiled. "I held it in my hand for hours the night I found it. Those who cannot resist become one with us. And in each, an Ift of old shares and moves. I am Torry but I am also Kelemark of Iftlanser. I was a tender of young growth and one learned in herbs and plant lore."

"Did none of you ever try to go back to the port—to the settlement?"

"Did you?"

"Yes. But that was a garth; they have a superstitious fear of the forest, of everything coming out of it. And the Green Sick to them is punishment for sin. Naturally they hunted me."

"But you, yourself, when you went there—did you want to stay? Were those humans *your* people?"

"No."

"We believe that this, too, was a part of the plan, that in becoming Iftin we were also implanted with a revulsion against our former kind. Thus, if the purpose of the planners was to rebuild their race, independent and truly Iftin once more, they deemed we must be apart from the species we once were. None of us can now force ourselves to return to the port—to any off-world holding. And the longer we are in the forest, the stronger that repulsion is. We are meant to recruit from them but not mingle with them."

"And this"—Naill's hand indicated their present situation—"what has this to do with it?"

"We don't know—more than we have learned from bits and pieces of memories. Your Ashla seems to know much more than the rest of us. She has taken on the Ift portion of some priestess or seeress of the last days. There is a force here—long hostile to the Iftin. It is stirring again because the Iftin also are reviving through us. As to what It is—or why It keeps us here"—Torry spread his hands—"we are not sure at all."

"The space suit?"

Torry was silent for a moment. "Your guess is as good as mine. I will say this much. I do not think any normal man wears that thing—though it is off-world and of a type I have worn myself."

"What are the boundaries of this place?" Naill wanted to know.

"We have a long narrow strip of forest, running for a good space north and south. There's that wall you came over, and beyond it all crystalline growth. We've explored in there at night. But we found nothing save the stairway and those walls and corridors none of which follows any pattern or sense we can determine."

"And that is all? Then where is this Thing in control?"

"We haven't been able to locate It. As far as we can discover, the crystal growth simply runs on and on. And we dared not follow it too far for fear of being caught out there in the day. Our night sight is limiting."

"So you've just accepted imprisonment, then?" Naill was once more amazed at what seemed a lack of enterprise on the part of the captives.

Torry smiled, a grim curve of lip. "We appear quite spineless, don't we, Renfro? But not quite. The way out is not always the most open. As you will see in due course."

"Ayyar—" Ashla came into the tree house carrying a holder improvised from a leaf. She showed him its contents. "Sa-san berries. Ripe sa-san berries here!" She shook three of the plump, red-black fruit, each as big as his thumb, into his hand. "There was a voice once in the Wind Forest." Her eyes were dreaming as she remembered. "Ah—how sweet its flowers smelled in New Leaf time!"

"Illylle," Torry said, "you remember a great deal, do you not?"

"Much, much, but still not enough!" Her dreaminess faded, she looked a little lost. "I thought—believed—that together we could break through, find what we lost. There was Jarvas, who had been Mirrormaster..." Her lost expression deepened. "But he was not enough Jarvas, he was too much Pate Sissions—and so we could not do it. And the rest of you—all different—different times, different powers. Perhaps it is the Turning of the Leaves which has made it so."

"The Turning of the Leaves, Illylle?" Sissions had followed her inside, and had taken one of her hands in his. "What is that?"

There was a small pucker set by impatience on

her forehead. "There was the Blue Leaf when the world was young and the Iftin were strong in their might. Then did Kymon come to this place and strive with That Which Abides, and the Oath was taken between Power and Power. None of us here were of that Leaf time—those mighty ones must have gone long, long ago, too far to be recalled. There came after the Green Leaf and of that Leaf were you, Jarvas, though you seem to remember it not. And then there was a lessening and a trial of the Oath. But still the Word held; though it was stretched thinner with time, it was still a tie.

"Third was the Gray Leaf, and that was the time of ending in which Illylle dwelt and he who is here as Derek but was then Loktath, a Sea Lord, and Ayyar—who was Captain at the First Ring of Iftcan. And that was a dark, dark time, for the people were few and they were tired with many years—and the children of the race were fewer yet. Then the Larsh, who had not said the Oath, gathered and marched. At last the end came, and the leaves fell. Thus we came together—not of one age or life—and united we cannot raise the Power as I had hoped."

These men were all older than he, Naill reflected, and, as Illylle's memories seemed to imply, they had once been of consequence in Iftcan. He was Naill Renfro, a worldless wanderer, lately a slave laborer. But a certain defiance rising in him made him speak now: "There is more than one heritage of power—" He was that far when he paused, a little shaken because they were all

staring at him now. "We have a double heritage."
He pushed on quickly. "And there is the space suit,
made by our own kind. The suit could only come
from a ship—no matter what wears it now—and
the ship was also ours."

Pate Sissions smiled. "All very true. Torry, how
is that arm of his? Is he ready for a journey?"

"If he takes reasonable care. Healing was quick,
as usual."

"Then I think it is time we move." He glanced up
at the tree bole around which this hut was
fashioned. "Iftscar may be a natural insulation
against arousing *that*." His hand pointed to the
strip of forest outside. "Only tonight there is a
stirring—I feel it. *That* may not know any more
about us, but It senses something. It is uneasy—
awake—"

"Yes!" Illylle interrupted. "That is the truth! It
stirs—and It knows Its power and how to use it!"

Whatever she and Pate Sissions were able to
pick out of the air was not discernible to the rest,
but their sincerity in believing it existed could not
be denied.

"We were very close to breakthrough last time,"
Monro observed. "And it is yet early evening—we
have the whole night before us."

They were gathering up the few furnishings of
the tree house, filling skin bottles with water,
making small packs of dried berries and nuts. It
would seem they did not intend to return. Naill
accepted one of the packs, slung it across his
shoulder, but asked no questions. He judged that

they were about to carry out some long-projected plan, as the amount of their food supplies, the extra water containers, meant a journey of some duration.

Sissions led the line of march with Ashla behind him. She was seldom far from the man she had named Jarvas and claimed as "Mirrormaster." Then came Derek, Torry and Naill, while Monro brought up the rear. Their weapons were three swords and two spears. Something in Naill questioned the assurance with which Sissions pushed ahead.

Shade of trees gave way to a patch of open, and there the wall of the valley was not glassily coated but rose as a stark white rock broken by a fault from which the stream ran. Sissions splashed into the water which rose to his knees, stooped head and shoulders to pass into the cave from which it flowed. And in turn they copied his move.

The stream bed offered smooth footing but the current was fast, pushing against them. They were not long in the water, but climbed to a ledge to crawl on hands and knees along a wet surface. As they drew away from the entrance, even their night sight did not serve them well and Naill marveled that the others had ever found this path.

The ledge brought them at last well above the waterline, and finally Torry drew Naill to his feet, keeping one hand on his shoulder to steady and guide him. Then they were out in a wide space where there was a dim gray light. Two sides of that area were coated with the slick crystal; the rest of the walling was rough stone, wrenched and broken as by some explosion or settling of the earth in a quake.

Light filtered through from well above their heads where on one of the crystalline walls was a narrow slit, coated with transparent material. To reach that slit a ledge had been chipped along the nearest stretch of rock wall. But still a space remained to be bridged between that ledge and the slit.

Sissions climbed with the ease of one who had done it many times before. At the highest point of the ledge he slipped a fiber band about his waist, dropped loops of cording over points of rock, and leaned back against that frail support. His aim was to the left and out, at a height above his own shoulder, an awkward angle at which to work. His tool was one of the swords. With swing curtailed by his position, he aimed the point of the sword into the lower end of the slit, picking time and time again at the same portion of sealing material. Four swings . . . five . . . a full dozen and he rested.

"Any luck?" Monro called. "Want one of us to spell you?"

"There was a give on that last punch. Let me try just once more."

His muscles moved visibly under the rags of the forest jerkin. The sword point thudded home with an effort Naill himself could somehow feel. And— went through!

The crackle of the breaking was loud. They could see a net of cracks spread across the surface. Someone gave a cry of triumph. Sissions struck again and there was no more resistance. A rain of splinters cascaded down, and wind—clear wind—whistled through the opened window.

"Rope!" Sissions' demand was curt. Derek was already climbing with a heavy coil of vine fiber wreathed about his shoulder.

They were a long time making that fast, testing its securing over and over again. Then Sissions unlinked his support belt, to resnap it to the rope. He gave a small jump, and his hands closed on the lower rim of the slit. In a moment he was up in it, perched on the edge looking out.

"How is it?" Monro called.

"As far as I can see clear—and"—Sissions' head turned as he looked straight down at Naill—"your ship's waiting out there, Renfro."

He dropped forward, out of their sight while the rope was payed out between Derek and Monro. The former astronavigator followed, then Torry—Ashla—Naill—with Derek steadying the rope and seeing them all through the slit before him.

The rock wall through which the window broke was part of a ridge for another valley. But the land below was not crowded with crystal growths—it was bare sand and rock. In that sand a ship posed on its fins, straight and tall. Whoever had piloted her in for that landing had made it a perfect three-point one, and she had stood undisturbed ever since, by all outward signs.

Her hatch was open and the entrance ramp was run out. There was a tall drift of sand about the foot of that ramp, and the rocket scorch of her set-down was no longer visible on the ground about her fins.

They advanced on the old ship cautiously. Naill gathered that they had spied upon her from the window slits over a period of several work nights. She was a Class-C Rover Five. Rover Five! That made her at least a hundred years old. She might have passed through many ownerships and, while she might have been considered too old to blast on the inner lanes, she was still spaceworthy for the frontier. Perhaps she had been a Free Trader. There was no service insignia symbol on her hull, and she was too small for a transport or regular freighter.

"Dead." Monro stood at the foot of the ramp.

"Maybe so," Sissions agreed. "But was she stripped? If not—"

If not, more suits—supplies of a kind that would take them across the waste, weapons better than the swords and spears. Monro was on his way up the ladder, the others strung out behind him. Did it hit them all at once—or were some more immune than others?

Ashla cried out and stopped, clinging to the handrail with a grip that made her knuckles into pale knobs. She wavered, almost fell. A moment later Sissions echoed her wordless protest with a spoken "No!"

It beat against them all. The revulsion Naill had known at Kosburg's was here a hundredfold the stronger. To advance was to fight against his churning insides for every inch. Distaste—no; this was a horror of disgust!

They swayed, held to the rail. Ashla went down, edging past Derek, past Torry, on her hands and knees. Monro kept his feet but he was swaying as he turned to descend. Sissions stumbled behind. Naill gripped the support so tightly with his good hand that the metal bit into his flesh. He was first in line now and he held there, facing the open door of the space lock.

His body fighting his will, he began to pull himself along—not down but up!

EIGHTEEN   JUDGMENT DELIVERED

He was Naill Renfro. There was no Ayyar, no Iftin, in him! He was Naill Renfro, and this was only a spaceship—like his father's.

Suit racks—empty. Naill steadied himself against the corridor wall with one hand. Dust was soft under his skin boots. The smell of age—of emptiness.... He was Naill Renfro exploring an old ship. So—no suits. But there could be other things here adapted to their needs. He pulled himself on, keeping his thoughts rigidly fixed on those needs and his human off-world past.

Arms cabinet—also empty. A second disappointment. This spacer appeared to be stripped of everything that could serve survivors. Perhaps the landing had been an emergency one and the crew had departed with their equipment, never to return.

No weapons—no suits. Naill leaned his head against the wall and tried to think clearly, to remember the stores on the *Lydian Lady* and where they had been. It was a struggle to do that with the awful horror of this place tearing at his mind, churning in his stomach, rising in a sour taste at the back of his throat.

Where now? He shuffled on. There was one more—just one more place to check. Naill was sure he did not have the strength to venture any farther into the spacer, to climb to another level. Here! He lunged and his good hand pressed on the panel of the compartment he sought. Here were the tools, the supplies for outer-skin repairs. The inner layout of the ships had not changed so much over the years that they were not arranged in the same general pattern. He forced the panel open.

His cry of triumph echoed hollowly down the passageway. Then he had them in his hand, the protective goggles to be worn while using a wield ray. Their key to freedom? Holding those tight to his chest, Naill wavered down the passage, came into the open and descended the ramp.

"What—?" Sissions met him.

"Listen..." Naill had the dim beginnings of a plan. He waved the goggles at the former Survey man. "With these on, the sun can't be too bad."

"One pair only—there are six of us." Torry joined them.

"One man leading, wearing these," Naill explained. "The rest of us blindfolded, linked together, by rope if need be. We could take turns with the goggles."

Sissions had those now. "It might work! How about it, Ladim?"

The former medico took them in turn, snapped the protective lenses over his eyes and looked about him.

"Can't be sure, of course, until we try. Used at short intervals, taking turns as Renfro suggests...well, we may never have a better chance. Though how far we have to travel west before we find any decent cover—"

"Not west!" That was so emphatic that they all turned to face the girl. She had been sitting on the ground at the foot of the ramp, but now she stood erect.

"Westward *That* will be watching...waiting. ...Once *It* knows we have escaped—"

"South to the river, then?" Derek asked uncertainly. The girl appeared so sure of what she was saying that it impressed all of them.

"No!" Her answer was as determined as before. "East!"

"Back to Iftcan?" began Monro.

Naill had been studying Ashla. She was gripped by that half-fey mood he had seen her display so many times during their flight together. Just as he had pulled on his human heritage to dare the ship, so was she now pulling herself into her Iftin personality.

"Not Iftcan." Her head moved slowly from side to side. "The day of Iftcan is done. That forest was withered and will leaf no more. We must go to the Mirror. This is laid upon us," she cried out fiercely, directly at Sissions. "We must go to Thanth!"

"I say get out of here and head west!" Derek protested.

"She's right about one thing," Torry cut in. "They—whoever or whatever controls this place— would expect us to do just that—west with no long way around. It might just be smarter to circle around by starting east, then south to the river."

"We go to Thanth!" Illylle repeated. And now Sissions added his will to hers. But not too completely: "East...for now."

They pointed eastward from the forgotten ship, hastening to make the most of the remaining hours of darkness. The valley wherein the old spacer had set down ended in a cliff up which they climbed, coming out on a waste of crushed crystal sand, facing, some yards away, the White Forest where moonlight flickered and sparked.

"No trail through that," Monro pointed out. "How will we know we're going straight and keeping east?"

"Those branches"—Sissions indicated the nearest "tree"—"are all right-angled and they grow in an established pattern. See this one and that? We keep our eye on the third branch up on every second tree. Let's get through this before sunup if we can."

It was a strange way to trace a path through the crystalline wilderness, but the Survey Scout, trained to note just such oddities, was right. The third branch on every second tree pointed in the same direction—a long glittering finger to the east. And they took turns watching for it, the rest shielding their eyes against too much of the reflection and glitter.

Naill was in the lead on his turn as pathfinder when he saw mirrored on a trunk of a neighboring tree a dark patch which came into better perspective and stopped him short. In spite of the distortions of that reflected image, there could be no mistaking the space suit.

The fugitives clustered together, to stare at the broken vision on the surface of the pillar. How far away it might be they had no idea.

Illylle spoke first. "It is not moving."

"No. Could be that it is waiting for us to walk right up and get caught again," Monro commented.

"I think not." Sissions' head had turned from right to left and back again. He had glanced from the image on the tree to the other growths about them. "It is behind us and perhaps to the right. And it is not moving at all."

Torry gave a grunt. "Close to dawn now, I judge. That thing may believe there's no need for hurry, that it can round us up quickly enough when the sun rises. I'd say we'd best make tracks and fast."

Torry's suggestion was accepted. They did hurry their pace as best they could. And when they left the reflection of that space suit behind, it did not show again, though they kept watch for it. So the medico's guess could be right—the guardian of the White Forest saw no reason to hurry in pursuit.

When the fugitives paused again, it was to make their final preparations against the sun. Torry argued that because of his training and ability to judge properly the efficiency of the goggles, he must have first chance as guide. The rest tore strips from their clothing and adjusted blindfolds which were as light-reducing as they could make them, after linking themselves together with the fiber rope.

Their advance slowed to hardly more than a crawl with Torry supplying a running description of the ground ahead, warning of missteps and obstructions. In spite of that there were falls, bumps, painful meetings with crystal growths. It was a desperate try, and only the heartening assurances from Torry that they were making progress kept them to it.

"Sun's hit the trees," he reported laconically some time later.

They were all aware now of the heat of those rays on their bodies, of a measure of light working through their blindfolds.

"What results with the goggles?" Sissions asked hoarsely.

"No worse than moonlight—yet," Torry returned.

So they were working this far. But suppose that the wyte pack waited ahead? They could not fight those blindfolded. And that suit—was it tramping stolidly along behind them, ready to gather them

in as easily as it had netted Ashla and Naill back
on the borders of the waste?

"Ah ..." Torry broke off his stream of directions
with a small cry. Naill tensed and then relaxed as
the other added, "End of the wood ... open beyond.
And—I'm ready for relief."

They had drawn lots before they had started
and were linked on the rope in the order of those
lots. Naill's hands went out readily, felt the
goggles fall into them as Torry pulled his waiting
blindfold down over his own eyes. Adjusting the
lenses and pushing up his blinder was an awkward process, but a few moments later Naill
blinked out into a bright morning which the
treated goggles turned into a bearable blaze.

He hurried to help Torry and the others on the
rope and then faced into the open country. It was
barren rock and sand—the sand running in
sweeps as if it were the water of dry rivers. And one
of those sandy streams, while thick to plod
through, ran east to give them smoother footing.
Naill plowed toward that, towing his line of
followers.

How far were they now from the valley of the
ship? Naill had no idea of how much ground they
had covered. He glanced back at intervals, each
time expecting to see the suited sentry emerge from
the blinding glitter of the White Forest, just as he
listened for the snarling cry of the wyte pack.

The river of sand, which had seemed a good road
away from the Forest, did not serve them long, for
it took a sharp turn to the north, and Naill was
faced with the fact that they must somehow make

their way up along a ridge. They rested, drinking sparingly of their water, eating nuts and dried berries.

"No reason to think it was going to be easy," Monro commented. "My turn to take over now. Maybe—if we went up one at a time—me helping—"

Naill's hands were fumbling with the goggles when he saw Ashla move.

"Wait!" Her word was an order. She was facing toward the Forest, which was now but a glittering spot behind them.

"*It*—stirs! *It* knows! Now *It* wonders ... soon *It* will move!" Her hands were fists. Naill could see only her lips, tight and compressed below the edge of her blindfold.

Sissions was on his feet, too. "Illylle is right. Pursuit will come."

"We can't run and we can't fly. Looks as if we've had it," Monro commented.

"No!" The protest came from the girl. "Now!" She whirled about to Naill as if she could see him through her blindfold. "This is my time to lead!"

"Not your turn—"

"This is not a matter of turns—or of anything but the knowing. And I have the knowing, I tell you! This is the time."

Sissions spoke. "Give her the goggles." The tone of that order overruled Naill's rise of protest.

His own blindfold was in place again when she spoke. "I am ready. Now we link hands,—we do not hold the rope."

Her own fingers tightened about his. He reached

out his left arm with caution, groped for Monro's
hand. Then...

Naill had no words to actually describe what
was happening, and Ayyar recognized it only
dimly as a flow of the Power. But it was as if he
could see—not physically but mentally—that
through him flowed an awareness of his surround-
ings which was coming not by the way of his own
senses, but from the girl, to pass along that line of
men hand-clasped together.

So linked, they began a scramble up and out of
the sand river and across the ridge beyond. Naill
could sense, too, the strain and drive that worked
in Ashla. Yet she kept going and they followed, at a
better pace than they had held since sunup.

"*It* has learned." Her voice was low and hoarse.
"Now *It* will truly move! *Its* servants gather."

And Naill heard—as if from very far off—the
soulless wail of a wyte.

"Will with me!" That came as a plea from her.
"Iftin warriors, Mirrormaster, Sea Lord—once you
all stood blade and power against That Which
Abides. Now will with my will, fight with those
wills as you did with your blades in a leaf time now
gone!"

Naill could not guess what response she aroused
from the others. But in him there was a glow of
anger and above it a wild, fierce determination to
stand against the Enemy. He shouted a long-
forgotten battle cry and did not know he mouthed
it, for now he was not hand-linked to a company of
fugitives; he was marching with his men, going to

the First Ring of Iftcan. And in him pride and belief were no longer dim but fiery bright and clear as the green spark that had tipped his blade to open the Guard Way of the Mirror.

Iftcan and his vision of the waste melted into one, fitting together so that green growth merged with rock, fertile forest soil with sand. And he was Ayyar as Ayyar had been in the greatest days of his life.

"The Mirror Ring—oh, my brothers—there is the Mirror Ring!" Illylle's voice cut through Naill's dream, and the vision she now saw fitted over the vision of Iftcan's Tree Towers—gray mountain with over it a patch of cloud growing and spreading to cut away the glare of the sun. They were all running, speeding across ground they did not see with their eyes.

Then—the Enemy struck! Heat—light—something akin to lightning cracked in their faces. That brooding fear Naill had felt waiting beyond the walls encasing the Mirror Road took on body—strength. The wailing of the wytes was no longer distant. And his long-ago battleground became here and now.

Why he did it he could not have answered sensibly, but he flung back his head, raised his face to a sky from which, through the fold of cloth, came a searing, baking heat. Then Naill called—not only with voice, but with mind, with every part of him. And the shrill "hooooorrruuuur" of that call carried, echoed and re-echoed.

"On—on!" That was Illylle's demand. Somehow

she was keeping them moving, summoning up
their will, their strength, projecting for them the
road they must take.

There was a roll of sound—a muttering along
the distant reaches of the sky. A puff of wind blew
in their faces, swirling up sand and grit to score the
skin. But it was not the furnace blast of the waste;
it was cool, carrying with it the smell of the forest.

And with the wind rode other things—feathered
things—hooting, protesting, yet coming. Wheel-
ing, dipping above those who ran, the quarrin kind
had answered Naill's summoning—not only
Hoorurr, but perhaps all of his species still holding
to the shadows and glades of Iftcan. The fugitives
could not see them, but they felt the impact of the
quarrin thoughts, heard through the wind the
sound of their wings. Three times the birds circled
the runners, and then they dropped behind to
where the wytes howled on a fresh and open trail.

The heat about them was the heat of anger. It
had been so long since That Which Abode had
roused to full participation in any struggle that *It*
was sluggish, unable to summon quickly old
strengths and powers. That was what saved them.
For had *It* struck earlier with the pressure *It* could
exert, they would have been stamped to nothingness in the dust of the waste.

"On—up!" Illylle's battle cry was a hacking sob.
Naill's hand dropped hers; flung out his right arm
and closed it about her waist. She was stumbling,
hardly able to keep her feet. But before them was
the barrier wall of the Mirror Road, and they had
met it where the rocks were as high as his head.

"Here!" He drew all the runners together with a call as he held up the girl, felt her wriggle in his hold. Then she was out of his grasp, gone—and out of his mind in the same move. A curtain had fallen between them.

"Over this!" Naill pictured in his own mind for the others the barrier about the road as he had seen it days ago. He stood with his hand on the rock wall, drawing each in turn to it, starting them to climb.

The wytes cried very closely now, their hunting bays broken by snaps, snarls—as if they fought. Naill guessed that the quarrin harassed that portion of the enemy forces.

The invisible power was the worst. Naill was thrust back and back—pulled from the roadway which he knew meant safety. Another step and he would be lost in his blindness. The heat bit into his brain, spread a blasting numbness down nerve and muscle.

Out of somewhere came a rope; a noose settled about his shoulders, jerked tight about his arms, tight enough to wring a gasp of pain from him. Now the pull was in the opposite direction. Naill stumbled and spun, breathless, only half conscious of the struggle.

> "Dark the seed, green the Leaf—
> Iftin power, Iftin belief..."

Had he said that, thought it? Had it come from him at all? A second in which to wonder, a moment of release from pressure growing intolerable, then with a bruising crash his body brought up against the rock wall of the road. He climbed—to fall into a swift stream of cool air and the welcoming hands of his companions.

The roll of thunder grew into a mighty beat of sound. Naill dragged off his blindfold and followed the others as they ran along the road. Above them was a gray ribbon of cloud, the edge of a mighty sunshade which stretched from the east as if it had its birth in the sky above dying Iftcan.

There stood the gate of the Guard Way. No sword had been drawn to open it this time, but the symbol on the keystone glowed green. The stairs—they took those stairs still at a breakneck pace, halting only when they reached the shelf over-hanging the Mirror.

A storm was coming, such a storm as had beaten the forest when Naill sheltered in Iftsiga. No wind reached into the basin which held the Mirror, yet the water was troubled. It moved in ripples around and around, rising with each stir of that circling.

Forces were gathering: forces such as Naill Renfro had never known—forces Ayyar held in awe.

Illylle moved a little away from the rest. She had swept off the goggles, stood watching the circling of the water.

"There has been a seeding. There is now a growing—soon will come the Leafing. But without the seeds, there will be no Leaf! If a Leaf is willed—protect the seeds and the growing. Give us now

Your judging. Shall the seeds endure until the Leafing?"

Was that an invocation of something— something utterly opposed to that which they fled—something that was the very life of Janus? Naill believed it to be so. And they stood to witness the answer to her appeal.

Up and up the water raced about the sides of the Mirror frame. It lapped against the edge of the ledge on which they stood, yet none of them retreated. Naill felt no fear. Once more he seemed on the edge of a great discovery. The time might not yet be fully ripe, but someday it would—and he was a part of it!

The first of those waves touched the peaks that cradled the Mirror—touched, lapped, spilled over. Faster and faster the water swirled. It was now ribboned and laced with green foam, spun by the speed of its boiling. Over through a dozen—two dozen—channels poured that flood, fountaining out into the waste beyond the boundaries of the Mirror frame. The wind howled, the clouds broke, pouring down a second kind of flood.

Under that deluge the fugitives gasped and reeled, but they did not seek shelter. It was a growing rain, a rain to encourage sprouting seeds—new life.

Lightning...lashes were laid in whip lines across the sky to the west. There was an answering blast there—a white glare flaring skyward as if to dry the clouds instantly of their water burden. There was terrible consuming anger to strike them, even this far away, as a wave of expanding energy. Then the rain closed down. The Mirror continued to pour its substance out and down to water the desert plain.

How long did that continue—the Mirror spilling, the clouds emptying rain? A few hours—a day? Naill could not have told. He was only aware that in time there was an end to that fury. Clouds parted. Stars shone serene in the sky. Still they were together on the ledge above a now quiet Mirror. And they were awed and small before a power far greater than they could imagine.

"We have much to learn." Jarvas who had been Pate Sissions spoke first.

"We have much to do." That was Torry, again Kelemark.

"*It* has not conquered—this time." Naill-Ayyar's hand was on his sword as he faced west.

He who had once been Monro and was now wholly Rizak smiled. "Nothing is ever too easy, if it is worth the winning—and the holding."

But Illylle smiled and hummed gently.

Naill-Ayyar knew that song; the words to fit the tune dropped into his mind one by one. It was very old—older than Iftcan, that song—for Iftcan's Tree Towers had been evoked and nourished from saplings by its singing. That was the Song of the First Planting.

"There shall be again a city." She broke the song to prophesy what they all knew in their hearts would come to pass. "And it shall rise where there was desolation. And the Oath shall be spoken once again. For the Iftin are replanted and the Nation shall grow—though the seeds were not of this world. There has been a judging and a judgment. We shall see a Fourth Leaf come into full greatness. But all growth is slow, and the way of the gardener is never without battle against destruction from without." She began to sing again—the song which was only for the Mistresses of the Planting. They listened to her almost greedily.

She walked ahead, began to descend the stairway leading to the plain and the night. Behind they followed eagerly.